W9-COU-002

PAX

JOURNEY HOME

SARA PENNYPACKER

PAX
JOURNEY HOME

ILLUSTRATED BY
JON KLASSEN

THORNDIKE PRESS
A part of Gale, a Cengage Company

Thorndike Press, a part of Gale, a Cengage Company.

Thorndike Press® Large Print Middle Reader.
The text of this Large Print edition is unabridged.
Other aspects of the book may vary from the original edition.
Set in 16 pt. Plantin.

LIBRARY OF CONGRESS CIP DATA ON FILE.
CATALOGUING IN PUBLICATION FOR THIS BOOK
IS AVAILABLE FROM THE LIBRARY OF CONGRESS.

ISBN-13: 978-1-4328-8893-0 (hardcover alk. paper)

Published in 2021 by arrangement with HarperCollins Children's Books, a division of HarperCollins Publishers.

Printed in Mexico
Print Number: 01   Print Year: 2022

To Donna Bray,
for taking such fine care of the foxes

— S.P.

Pax ran.

He always ran — nearly a year after he'd last been caged, his muscles still remembered the hex wire.

This morning the running was different, though. This morning the fox ran because below the hard, matted forest floor, below the crusts of snow that remained in the deepest pine-shades and below the wafers of ice lacing the puddles, he smelled it: spring. New life surging *up* — up from the bark and the buds and the burrows — and the only possible response to *up* was *go*.

And then suddenly he stopped. Rabbit.

Bristle was always hungry these days.

Pax canted toward the scent and found the warren. It had been abandoned only hours before. It held two kit carcasses, one dead many days, one lifeless a single night.

This was the third place in as many days that Pax had come upon dead young. The first, a field mouse burrow, held an entire litter. He had brought home the freshest body, but Bristle's snout wrinkled in disgust.

The second was a chipmunk nest. Bristle had refused the meal of dead pups, too, so Pax didn't bother with the rabbit kits. Instead, suddenly tired, he turned for the Deserted Farm that he, Bristle, and Runt had claimed since leaving the place where Runt had lost his leg.

Bristle wasn't in sight, but she was near. He trotted along her trail to an old shed. A hole had been tunneled under its steps, freshly scraped dirt scattered all around. Pax followed her scent inside.

Bristle was curled at the back of the new den, her bright fur clumped with sand. She opened one sleepy eye to her mate, then settled her face back onto her paws.

Pax was baffled. The morning air was already warming and held no threat of storm. Even more perplexing, there was a scent in the den he had never encountered before, but that he knew as well as his own. It was of Bristle, but it was not Bristle.

He nosed her neck, asking her to track the air. *New?*

Yes, new. Us.

Pax still did not understand.

Bristle rolled onto her back and stretched out her round belly. *Kits. Soon.* Then she curled back into the clean sand.

Pax watched her every breath until she fell asleep.

He backed out of the den, gave a single bark.

And then he ran. This time he ran because if he didn't, he would burst.

Peter crouched over the offending floorboard and traced the ridge that rippled all the way down. Vola had said the boards were flat enough, he could begin sanding, but he wanted them perfect when she saw the floor finished, not just flat enough.

He adjusted the wheel of the plane until the blade projected only enough to shave off veneers thin as paper. He could make a single thicker cut, but layer by layer would do a better job.

Peter liked planing — maybe best of all the skills he'd learned building the cabin. The plane was a real muscle tool, not like a screwdriver, say. You used your whole body with a plane. A tool for a man, not a boy.

He positioned it over the end of the board, wrapped his right hand over the knob and eased his weight onto it, then began to guide the plane forward with his left. The hundred-year-old yellow pine, salvaged from a neighbor's barn, sheared off in an even curl that smelled as crisp as fresh-cut wood. He liked how wood was always ready to start over, and how —

Suddenly, the plane stubbed up short against a knot. Peter's pushing hand shot off the knob and he skinned the pad of his palm.

He fell back on his heels, cursing. When was he going to learn? That was how knots were: sneaky, hiding under the surface. As the blood welled up and began to trickle down his wrist, the phrase struck: *blood and sweat*. He had dripped buckets of sweat all over this cabin. A little blood signature wouldn't be out of place. He pressed the cut to the board and watched a red flame leak out. The spreading stain looked like a fox's tail.

Peter jerked his hand back, shocked at how hard the memory hit. Last year, on his journey back to the place where he had been forced to abandon his pet fox, Pax, he'd nicked his calf so he could smear a fox-tail blood oath on his leg. *I will come back for you*, it vowed.

He pressed the wound to the center of his chest. Memories were so treacherous. Always lurking under the surface, ready to bushwhack you with a blade to the heart when you weren't careful.

He knew what he had to do to counteract this one. Kind of a penance he'd devised, actually. Every time he slipped up like this and thought about Pax, he made himself go through the same exercise. Best to do it right away.

Peter closed his eyes. He visualized the afternoon when he'd found a dead vixen by the side of the road. He went over all his steps in detail: picking up her stiff, muddy body; carrying it away in search of a place to bury it; noticing the sandy spot beside a stone wall and scraping out a shallow grave with his boot.

Although his chest was tightening the way it always did at this part, he made himself remember finding the opening to the fox den. It hurt to breathe now, but he

14

drew up the scene again: three dead kits and one shivering survivor.

He had reached in and lifted the live kit — a male, a little dog fox. He'd curled it snug against his chest, where it had filled a hollowness he hadn't known he was carrying. But now, for the penance, he spliced in a different scene: the thing his dad told him he *should* have done.

"It was meant to die with the rest of its family. The right thing to do would have been to make that be painless."

Holding the kit, Peter had been outraged. "Too late," he'd cried. "And I'm keeping him!"

His father had been irritated. But in his expression — for the first time, maybe — Peter had seen respect.

Now he could see that his father had been right. He should have put Pax out of his misery, and out of the pain he himself would cause them both five years later.

He finished the penance. No reaching in. Instead, he imagined himself wresting off one of the heavy capstones from the top of the wall and dropping it over the entrance to the den. And then immediately walking away without ever looking back.

Do it. Walk away. Don't look back.

All that pain he would have avoided.

Peter ran the sequence two more times. He'd read it took three times to reprogram your brain.

The penance was working. He thought of Pax less and less. If he could avoid seeing Vola's raccoon, he could go days without remembering he'd ever had a pet.

He got up and put the plane away. His cut had stopped bleeding, but he would avoid the tool for a while. You couldn't give memory a way in.

He took a piece of canvas off a trough in the corner. In it he had piled dried moss, woodstove ash, and clay slurry. He mixed in some more water until he'd made a rough paste. Then he troweled some into a pail and began chinking the spaces between the logs on the north wall.

While he worked, he allowed himself to admire the cabin. He'd decided to build it back in September, when he'd come home from the first day of school and spread his books over Vola's kitchen table and seen how impossible the situation was. Vola's cabin was perfect for her, but it was too small for two. They'd agreed that he needed some space and some privacy, and she'd helped him design a place to sleep and study. Just ten by twelve — room enough for a bed and bureau, a desk and chair — its simplicity appealed to him.

He had felled the logs himself, sawed each to length and notched them. He'd cut every rafter and beam, shingled the roof and tarred it. Last week, he'd found three windows and a door in a junkyard and bought them with the money his grandfather sent each month. He would start framing them tomorrow after school.

Neighbors had helped raise the logs into place, but otherwise he'd done every job alone. Vola had guided him, of course, but she'd barely lifted a hand. That was the deal — he wanted to build something all himself — and she respected that. He liked that about her.

Just then, as if he'd called her up, he saw Vola walking down the path. She looked uncomfortable, tugging on her skirt as if she still hadn't gotten used to dressing up for her library days.

She stepped up onto the cinder block he'd placed at the doorway for her — she got around really well on her prosthetic leg, but tall steps were awkward — and knocked on a log. Another thing Peter liked was that she respected his space, too.

He spread a tarp to hide the unfinished floor and then waved her in. "How'd it go today?"

Vola smiled. "That little Williams girl is going to drive me nuts. But she's got a feel for the marionettes. Bea says hello. She ordered that new book on trees you wanted. I didn't think there was a book on trees left that you hadn't read. Oh, and I almost forgot. Someone put up a sign on the bulletin board. Puppies. Lab and spaniel were in the mix. I was thinking . . ."

Peter's breath went shallow. He turned away. "No." Now Pax was in his head again. He picked up the trowel. "I have to get back to work."

"I was just thinking maybe a little company when you start spending time out here . . ."

"No!" The sharpness of his voice surprised him.

Vola stepped back. "All right. It is too soon. I understand."

Peter doubted that Vola did understand, since he didn't understand himself. All he knew was that the idea of having a pet again made it hard to breathe.

She smiled a conciliatory smile.

Peter nodded and slapped a load of slurry onto the wall. He wished she would leave. He had to run the penance right away, or the memory would grow roots. He smoothed the slurry along the log.

Vola's smile faded. "I told you yesterday, don't seal it up so tight."

Peter bit his cheek and spread on another thick band of chinking. "Keep out the cold."

"You'll keep out the air and the light."

He stuffed the chinking deep into the gap.

"People die without light and air, boy," Vola said in a quieter voice.

"I know," he said without looking up. "People die from the cold, too."

Pax paced.

The last week had been warm, but tonight the midnight air sparkled with frost. A full moon tugged at him, but Bristle's pull was stronger.

She'd entered the den below the shed at dusk, her belly swaying. Pax had heard her circling, trying to settle, then digging at the floor, then circling again. He had poked his snout in once when he heard her panting with effort, but she'd growled at him. *Do not enter. But stay near.*

Since then he'd patrolled the ground around the shed and the broad saucer of meadow, greening with new shoots, in front of it. For hours, he'd encountered no intruders, but now he heard the approach of a familiar gait.

Bristle's brother moved with an odd three-footed roll after losing a hind leg the spring before. But he'd become a fine hunter — his eyes and ears seemed to have sharpened to compensate for the loss of quickness — and now he emerged from the brush with a fat quail in his jaws, which he dropped at the den entrance.

Runt's ears pricked toward the rustling inside.

Before Pax could warn him, he ducked in. Pax heard a hiss, and a few seconds later, Runt stumbled out backward, whimpering. He slunk off to flop down at the base of an oak a safe distance away.

Pax followed and lay down beside Runt. Runt curled his tail over his snout and closed his eyes, but Pax stayed alert, gaze trained on the den. He would not try to enter until Bristle invited him — he had encountered her sharp teeth before — but he felt a need to protect her tonight.

As dawn began to lighten the sky, a blood scent drifted over.

Pax flew to the den.

A wet heat rose into the cold air. The blood it carried was not from a wound, not from death. This was life blood, pulsing and new. And it demanded his presence.

He darted inside.

Bristle was licking three squirming bodies. The kits were dark and slick. As his eyes adjusted, Pax saw tiny legs stretch out from the pile. Tiny pink paws curled, tiny pink noses wriggled, and tiny pink ears flicked with new life.

Bristle purred. *Ours. Safe.*

Pax dropped to the floor and curled himself around his family. Three tiny hearts beat into his own. *Safe. Ours.*

"I decided."

Peter's grandfather looked up from the television with a grunt of annoyance. "Decided what?"

"The ashes. I'm going to take them. Sir."

The old man's eyes darted to the cardboard box on the mantel over the woodstove.

The box sat beside the four framed photos that had been lined up there for as long as Peter could remember. First one: his grandfather at eighteen, decked out proud in army gear on a doorstep with the great-grandparents Peter had never met. Next, his grandfather getting married

to the grandmother Peter could barely remember. The third was a photo of the couple beaming over a baby who turned out to be Peter's father. And the last was a picture of Peter himself — a big-eared little boy in a suit, standing between his mother and father, grandfather to the side. The four photos had always seemed to be daring you to believe their improbable stories — his grandfather's life held a family.

His grandfather narrowed his eyes and Peter knew that he was weighing his claim on the ashes. Who should have what was left of a man? The man's father or his son? Peter drew himself up taller.

The old man swiveled his beat-up armchair, crossed his boots. He turned down the volume, leaving the game-show host gesturing wildly in silence. "What are you thinking to do with them?"

"They belong with my mother. Her grave." Peter looked his grandfather in the eye, something he usually avoided because whenever he saw himself reflected there, he always came up short.

He hardened his gaze. He owed this to his mother. Lately, he'd felt strangely guilty, as if she wanted something from him and he'd been failing her. Getting those ashes next to her — that had to be it.

The old man worked his mouth, as if trying out an argument. Then he looked down to the arm of the chair and scraped at a scab of dried food with his thumbnail. And Peter knew he had won.

"Fair enough," his grandfather said. "When you going to go?"

"Whenever school lets out, I guess. It'll be early this year, so kids can join the Junior Water —"

"I know. Water Warriors. A joke — bunch of do-gooders, prancing around pretending to be real military."

Peter didn't feel that way. He agreed with Vola that it was exactly the right thing to do: repurpose the training, the equipment, and the workforce of the military to repair the damage done in the war. And the Junior Water Warriors seemed like a good idea, too — enlisting kids to help clean the water. He bit his lip, though. He wanted those ashes.

His grandfather hauled himself up with a groan and went to the mantel. But instead of picking up the cardboard box, he pulled a brown envelope from underneath it. "This came. Took 'em long enough."

From across the room, Peter recognized the military insignia. "Oh. They determined . . ." He stopped and swallowed hard. "Circumstances of . . ."

"They did. You want to know?"

Peter started to nod, but the look on the old man's face froze him. His dad hadn't died a hero in combat, that much was obvious. Which they already knew, otherwise why the big mystery for six long months? He'd been hit by enemy mortar a hundred miles from his base, but that was all they'd been told. Not having a final answer somehow made it less real, and that was okay with Peter. "No. I don't want to know."

"Maybe you do. Yeah, maybe you need to read this. Because your father died of stupid." He crossed to Peter and thrust the envelope in his face like a threat. "You read what's in here, learn yourself a lesson."

Peter pushed the envelope away. "He died in the war. That's all." He'd already said that to everyone at school. He was getting used to saying it. People died all the time in war. No details needed.

"Suit yourself, don't read it, then. But you hear me now. Don't get too thick with other folks."

"Yes, sir. Don't worry, I won't."

"Don't go soft. Got it?"

"Yes, sir. I've got it." Peter walked to the mantel and picked up the box. It was heavier than it looked, but still it felt too light to hold all that was left of a big man. He tucked it under his arm and hardened his bicep around it. He crossed to the door. "I better get back to Vola's. It's getting dark."

"Wait."

Peter stopped, a hand on the doorknob. Maybe his grandfather was going to offer to go with him to spread the ashes. That would be okay. Ever since he'd chosen to live with Vola, when his grandfather looked at Peter it seemed he wanted to spit. Maybe on a trip like this they could patch things up, get to know each other better. If he wanted to come along, Peter would say yes.

But that wasn't it. His grandfather walked up behind him and slid something into Peter's backpack. "Take this, too."

Without looking, Peter knew it was the envelope. He would throw it away later. He turned the doorknob, but his grandfather still wasn't finished.

"People are tricky. You have to watch all the time."

"Yes, sir," Peter said as he opened the door to the cold, sharp air. "I'm watching all the time."

Pax sat on a boulder beside the path that led away from the shed. He dropped the mouse he'd brought home. He was tired from a night of hunting, and the sun was warm on his back, but he did not drowse.

His family was outside.

Bristle had begun carrying the kits up to the dish of sand at the den entrance on mild days. It was only a few quick steps back to safety, but Pax knew how suddenly a hawk could glide down or a coyote spring up. From this vantage point, he could see any danger coming up from the fields below the farmhouse, any from the sky.

This morning, the spring air carried only the friendly scents of wild things reclaiming the Deserted Farm: honeysuckle climbing over the shed's roof, clover narrowing the path, swallows and chipmunks nesting in the barn.

The spot had turned out to be a good home. The Broad Valley they'd come from had also been good. But war-sick humans had invaded and brought fire and chaos. This Deserted Farm, and the deserted farms all around, were better, because there were no humans at all.

Pax turned to watch the kits. Their movements perplexed him — staggering around, collapsing without warning, springing up in unpredictable hops — but he was drawn to them.

He could tell them apart now, even from a distance.

The largest, one of the males, moved like a bear cub. He would patrol the perimeter of the play area full of bravado, and then lumber back to his mother.

The smallest was a dog fox also. Skittish and hesitant, he darted under the step at the slightest noise or shadow.

The third kit — the female — always began marching off the sand and into the new meadow grass as soon as she emerged from the den. The tiny vixen carried her tail upright and her ears pricked determinedly forward.

Now, Pax watched her back out from the pile nursing at Bristle's belly. She blinked in the sunshine and sniffed every direction as if trying to decide which scent to follow, then headed down the path.

Bristle rose, caught her daughter by the scruff of the neck and deposited her back on the sand, then lay down. Immediately, the two dog foxes clambered back over to their mother, and immediately, the little vixen toddled back out.

Bristle got up again, sending her sons sprawling, and retrieved her daughter.

Pax watched as once more, the tiny adventurer squirmed out of the pile of fur to head down the path. This time, Bristle didn't follow. She flicked a glance toward Pax, and he understood.

He dropped from the boulder and stretched out alongside the path, a paw ready to sweep his kit to him as she passed.

She stopped once, twice, three times to investigate — a worm, an acorn, a falling feather — but each time, she lifted her head after a second and began to totter down the path again.

When she reached the spot where Pax waited, she stopped. She cocked her head and gazed at her father for a moment. Then she climbed over his foreleg, up onto the white ruff of his chest.

Pax rolled back to balance her, and she collapsed over his heart, as if she had been searching for that spot her entire life. Four legs splayed, tail straight up, she promptly fell asleep.

Pax lay perfectly still.

The little fluff of gray on his chest was nearly weightless, but he felt pinned to the ground as if the boulder beside him had rolled.

Whatever this kit needed, he would provide.

When Peter saw Vola start up the path
from the barn, he glanced around the cabin
floor one more time. Waxed and buffed
three times, the pine boards gleamed.

He threw open the door. The afternoon
sun poured onto a rectangle of floorboards, burnishing them to a deep honey
color, and he warmed with pride.

Vola stopped on the cinder-block doorstep, one hand on the jamb. "Well, finally I
am allowed to see," she said, taking in the
finished floor. Her eyes widened. "Oh,"
was all she said, but in the word was a
world of praise.

Peter stepped back. "It's dry. Come
on in."

Inside, she turned around and around, inspecting his work, the way he hoped she would.

Then she got to her knees — something that was still awkward, even with the good prosthetic. She ran knowing fingers over the joints. "Well. The apprentice surpasses the teacher."

"What do you mean?"

"You trued up the ends, butted them tight. That is where I would have left it — it is a floor. But you matched the grain. And countersinking the nails and filling the holes? I am impressed."

Peter turned his head to hide his grin, but not fast enough.

"No. You *should* be proud," she said, smiling with him. "You've earned it. You are making yourself a fine home."

Peter's grin disappeared. "This isn't my home."

Vola got herself up before she answered, as if she wanted the height. "Of course it is. You built it. Why do you think I had you do each job yourself?"

Peter shrugged. "So I would learn how to do all the steps. I asked you to let me do everything myself."

"That's right. But also so that you would know your home. In your hands, in your back and heart. You are in this cabin and it is in you."

"No. Doesn't matter. I'll sleep here and I'll study here while I'm staying with you, but this isn't my home. It's your land. It's your place here."

"Ah, the land. I see. Well, I've been meaning to talk to you about that. Now is as good a time as any."

She crossed over to the rough tool shelf he'd hung on the far wall and leaned against it. "You have lost a great deal for someone so young, Peter," she said as though she had practiced the words. "I am having papers drawn up to give you half of this property. I want you to know that whatever you do, wherever you go, whether I am alive or not, you have a place."

Peter reared back. Once, horsing around with some friends on a frozen river, he'd skidded out to where the ice had been thin. He still remembered sensing too late the cold dark water all around, waiting to swallow him. He felt that same kick of panic and dread now.

"You get the half closest to civilization, of course," she added with a rueful shake of her head. "I have not changed that much, eh?"

"I don't want it."

"I am looking ahead for you, Peter. You are almost fourteen. You will go. Maybe college. Maybe you will not come back, but if you do . . ." Vola spread her hands out to the cabin. "It's just a room now. But you add yourself a kitchen, bedroom in the back, looking out over the peach trees. And just because I don't want electricity, fancy plumbing, doesn't mean I would keep it from you."

"I don't want it."

She chuckled. "Well, fine. No electricity. For now, but we will see later, I think."

Peter turned his back to Vola. "No. I mean I don't want any of it. This place."

He heard Vola take a step toward him. "Half the people in this country would give their right arms for what we have here," she said. "Clean water, springing out of the ground. That is not likely to change anytime soon."

"I don't care about that."

"I think it is what your parents would want. To know you had a place that would keep you safe. That you love."

The panic, the dread was rising. Nameless, but rising. "I don't love anything here."

"But that is not true," Vola said quietly. "I have watched you in this forest, in that orchard. You love this land. I have watched —"

"I don't!"

"I have watched you working with wood. I have watched you build this cabin. I know love when I see it. You love it all."

"I don't love it! I don't need it. None of it. Not the land, not the wood, not this . . ." He looked around wildly, saw every traitorous job he had done here, skidding onto that thin ice. He picked up the hatchet and flung it into the floor. The blade splintered a bite out of the perfect gleaming wood. "Not this stupid place!"

"What is wrong, boy? What have I said?" Vola raised her arms toward him, and suddenly the nameless dread had a name.

Peter jumped clear. "You're not my mother!"

Vola flinched. She pulled her arms in and wrapped them around her chest. "I know that. I know that. I only meant . . ."

"I don't need anyone," Peter said, trying to walk back the sharpness of his words.

But the blow had been struck. Vola was looking at him as if she felt sorry for him, not for herself. Peter turned away from the sight. *Do it, walk away, don't look back.*

He heard her sigh and pull the hatchet from the torn pine. He heard her lay it on the shelf, and knew that the shaft was lined up straight with the other tools, blade in, the way she'd taught him. He heard her walk to the door, heard her footfall on the cinder-block step, heard her close the door behind her, and still he didn't turn around.

But when he heard nothing, he ran to the window.

Peter watched her walk down the path, walk away from him, with her back rigid. He doubled over. His chest hurt so much he thought he might die.

Pax meandered home, taking in the scents and sounds of the mild spring night. But when he came to the edge of the Deserted Farm, the thought of his young family urged him on faster, and he trotted through the last stretch of woods as the sky lightened with the coming dawn.

When the roof of the shed came into sight, he stopped. Yesterday, Bristle had enlarged the den for the growing kits, and the fresh sand sparked like frost on the grass. The fields below were peaceful. Still, Pax sank down to watch the surroundings.

The kits were beginning to venture farther from the den these days. Bristle wanted to bring them to the reservoir this evening, to teach them to drink on their own. He would go along, because it took both parents now to corral them on an outing.

Just then he caught a movement at the base of the shed steps. Pax felt his hackles rise, but then he saw: it was only a bit of fluff, moving with weightless jerks, not the low stealth of a hunter. One of the kits was outside alone.

Bristle would not allow this.

It was the little vixen, of course — the only one of the litter who ever defied her mother.

He watched her for a moment. She dipped her head to the ground, and then set out for the back of the shed, following her nose. From there, she stalked slowly, paw over paw, to the clump of shadbush, then veered out to the raspberry thicket.

It was the path Pax had followed when he'd left a few hours ago. His daughter was tracking him.

He called to her.

The kit spun in her tracks and mewed back. She began to bounce toward him in joyful little hops.

He hurried toward her also. He would chastise her for the disobedience, then carry her back into the den. But just as he reached the clearing, a span of muscled wings swept down. Outstretched talons tore through the soft darkness above her head.

Pax leaped. He caught the horned owl by its feathered thigh as it rose, but the bird had the kit in its talons.

The owl pecked at his face, but Pax did not let go.

He felt himself dragged as it beat its great wings. He twisted his hind legs upward and raked the bird's belly, but the owl held fast to its prize.

Pax clamped deeper and felt teeth crack hollow bone. He snapped his head hard. The owl shrieked and unlocked its talons.

The kit dropped, and the owl flapped off.

Pax checked his daughter all over. Except for double talon-piercings on each shoulder, she was unharmed, but she shook in terror.

He licked her wounds, he wrapped his body around her and let her wriggle into

41

the fur of his ruff, and still she shivered and her heart hammered.

Pax's heart beat hard also, from a different fear.

You must always look up. Danger from above can be silent.

The advice was not enough to protect her. Nothing would ever be enough.

8

"Come on. We're here to practice."

Peter jumped up, embarrassed. "Sorry, right." It happened every time. He never even missed television at Vola's, but when he went to Ben's house, he always collapsed in their family room and stared at it, slack-jawed, until Ben knocked his shoulder and reminded him of why they were there.

He scooped up his glove and followed Ben out the door.

Astrid, Ben's five-year-old sister, followed, too, as usual. Secretly, Peter had nicknamed her Echo. Not just because she copied everything her brother said or did, and not just because she was a smaller version of him — pale hair, freckled, and determined — but because somehow she was also *fainter*. As if she weren't quite there. As if this whole life thing was a toss-up for her, except for how much she adored Ben.

Outside, Ben picked her up and planted her on the porch steps. He put a bag of sunflower seeds beside her. "Watch this for us. And stay up here. We're going to be throwing pretty hard, okay?"

"Pretty hard, okay," she agreed.

Peter peeled off his sweatshirt. Spring had been coming on fast the past week. It was baseball weather. The driveway was rocky, perfect for practicing grounders. For a while they threw low and sharp toward each other, and mostly they caught the balls, no matter how unpredictably they spun out. It felt good to play with someone who loved baseball as much as Peter did, who could focus as hard. When they did miss, one called the other "Has-Ben" or "Petered-out" and that felt good too, because the corny joke was familiar now, after a year.

44

But then one grounder took a rogue bounce and hit the corner of the house and spun into the plantings. Ben went for it, and as he was trotting back, he called, "Westville won't know what hit them."

Peter pulled his glove off, pretended to adjust the lacing. "I'm not playing summer ball."

"What are you talking about?"

Peter picked up his own ball and snugged it into the glove. Practice would be over, because of what he had to say next. What he'd decided last night. "I'm signing up with the Junior Water Warriors."

Ben laughed. "No, you're not. They aren't coming here. Our water's okay. Come on, put your glove on." He ran back to his position.

"No. Listen. I know they're not coming here. I'm going there. I leave Saturday."

Ben grew still, a fist on his hip. "Going where?"

"Back to where I used to live." The idea had struck last night when he'd learned that the Water Warriors were scheduled to clean up a site in his old town. He didn't need Vola's offer of a home because he already had one. He would do a stint with the Junior Warriors there, and be within walking distance of his own house.

"But that's like, a hundred miles away."

"Three hundred."

"Vola's letting you?"

Peter shrugged. "I'm telling her tonight. But she'll let me."

Ben turned away and began tossing the ball up onto the garage roof.

Peter understood, because baseball was a language they shared, the throw and catch of it, the way they had learned to predict each other's moves, the way they could say real things, the hardest things, as long as they kept their eyes on the game. Right now Ben was saying, *Okay, I need a little time by myself with this news*.

Suddenly, Peter didn't want that. Ben had had his back since the first day Peter had walked into the school, all new-kid nerves and lonely without Pax.

"You could come, too," Peter said now, without thinking it through. "We can share a tent. I heard they let you drive Bobcats and stuff. There's canoeing, collecting samples, and —"

"I can't."

"Sure you can. As long as you're over twelve and your parents sign —"

"No. *I* can't." Ben nodded over to the porch steps, where his sister was shaking sunflower seeds onto her head. *Her operation*, he mouthed.

Astrid jumped off the porch and came running over, as if she knew she was being talked about. Ben dropped the baseball and drew her in close. He began pulling sunflower seeds out from her hair.

Peter took a step back. "Oh. You mean she might . . ."

Ben's arm tightened around his sister. "She'll be *fine*. But she would be scared without me there."

"I would be scared," Astrid repeated. But Peter saw that she was smiling. And it was Ben who looked terrified.

Right then it struck him with a jolt. He was immune. Yes, he had lost everything — mother, father, fox. Everything he'd ever cared about. But having lost everything, he had nothing left to lose.

At thirteen, life could never hurt him again.

"Be careful," he couldn't help warning his friend.

Ben looked up. "What do you mean?"

Peter noted how Ben had gathered his sister's hair at the roots so it wouldn't hurt as he tugged the shells out. It was too late for Ben.

But it wasn't too late for him. "Nothing." He pulled down the bill of his cap and ran to his bike. "See you around," he called, kicking off down the driveway.

"Wait," Ben called. "Maybe I could go if I'm back in time. . . ."

"Never mind. I don't want company anyway." *Do it, walk away, don't look back.*

Pedaling back to Vola's, he thought about how close he'd just come. A friend was the last thing he needed on his trip. Maybe a friend was the last thing he needed, period.

Vola tapped a spot on the newspaper map between them. "The Water Warriors are stationed here now. It's a reservoir, about fifty miles upriver of where you used to live."

Peter nodded, but didn't speak. In spite of what he'd said to Ben, and in spite of how he'd hurt Vola yesterday, he was still surprised that she hadn't put up an argument when he'd told her what he wanted to do. She'd been extra cautious around him all day, but "That's a long way away" was all she'd said. "But I understand."

Vola's finger traced a path down the map. "They're working downstream. When they finish at the reservoir, about a week maybe, they'll follow this river south."

Peter watched her finger come to rest on the spot where the river widened beside the old mill. It was the spot where last spring he had found Pax again after abandoning him. Where he had let him go for good. Where his father had helped rig the explosive that blew up that river, that tore the leg off that smaller fox. The spot where he had last seen them both, his father and his fox.

It would be a tough place to stay, but in return, he'd get a month on his own. And after that, he would go to his old home. He would feel safe there, he could figure things out. He would go to his mother's grave, spread his dad's ashes there, make that right for her.

"The whole area will be dangerous," Vola was saying. "You know how to make a solar still; always use the iodine drops. . . ."

Of course Peter knew all this — Water Safety was now a mandatory class in every school in the country. Besides, the Warriors were experts. He let her talk, though, because he knew she needed the reassurance.

"And just because you're in the middle of nowhere, don't assume the water is safe. The chemicals may have reached the aquifer. You come upon a pond, crystal clear, that's actually a warning sign."

"I know. It's clear because nothing can live in it."

"Look at this." She swept a hand over the map again. "They're reporting there are no young of any species in the whole area this year. The young can't survive the poisoned water."

Peter allowed himself to picture Pax, although it meant he'd have to run the penance again tonight. That was okay, he was getting used to it. The penance didn't hurt so much anymore. "Pax probably still lives around there. But he's not young. He'd be six now."

"I am not worrying about your fox, boy. I am worrying about you. The young of all species includes humans, you know. You must not take any chances."

"I know. I'll be careful." He stood up, folded the newspaper.

"One more thing. It won't be like it is here, where you can count on having what you need. Fill your cup whenever you can."

9

At high moon, Pax and Bristle set out with the kits for the reservoir.

The trip took a long time. The two little dog foxes insisted on stopping to investigate every new thing they encountered, and they encountered many new things: a leather boot, exotically scented; crunchy milkweed pods that released floating stars when pulled apart; skunk cabbage, which tasted as bad as it smelled. Startling discoveries at each turn.

The smaller one followed a beetle into a tangle of greenbrier. While Pax and Bristle were freeing him from the thorny vines, the larger one skittered off after a skunk waddling by, and Pax had to jump back to snatch him out of danger in time.

Only the little vixen gave them no trouble. If she left Pax, it was only to sniff or taste something he showed her. After a quick test of the novelty, she darted back under his chest, where she walked between his paws so that sometimes he tripped over her, slowing them down even more. Whenever he nudged her out to travel beside him, she looked up nervously so often she herself tripped.

The world was full — of both pleasures and dangers. Pax knew that he and Bristle must teach their kits everything they would need to know. *Yes, look up*, he agreed with his daughter. *But also look around.*

He showed her a pale green moth as large as her head, trembling against the papery bark of a birch tree. He showed her a hollow where the blackberries grew so thick that in summer they would stain her coat as she ate, and a field where apples would fall around her while she napped in the autumn sun. *There is bounty wherever you look.*

Presently they reached the chain-link fence that surrounded the reservoir, and Pax grew wary. The wire stirred deep memories of being caged, but it was the reservoir that made him uneasy.

Its vastness alone was a mystery: no matter how far along the shore he ran, he could see only water. He had never encountered such a body of water, where there was no shore *across*. And no other body of water he knew was bordered in places by long buildings and walls, so that its surface slapped against concrete, sounding angry.

Most confusing, it smelled of nothing. In his year of freedom, Pax had learned that water smelled of the life it traveled past. Rain-catch smelled of sky, and of the leaves it splashed upon. Rivers smelled of moss and silver-flash trout. Springs smelled of roots. But the water here traveled past no life at all: no fish swam in the depths, no crabs scuttled along the shallows, no clams studded the mud. Only dead reeds rimmed the shore.

Pax waited for Bristle and the other two kits to catch up, and then they slipped under a bent corner of wire.

As they approached the reservoir, Bristle growled an alarm. Pax flattened himself and ordered his family to follow his lead.

He edged forward until he had a good view.

Far up the shore, beside the buildings, he saw lights. *Stay. I will go to see.*

The little vixen whimpered as he crept out, but he ordered her to stay again, and to be silent, and she curled up close to her mother.

Pax trotted in a loop, staying downwind. As he neared, he smelled woodsmoke and heard wisps of human voices.

Unlike Bristle, Pax was not afraid of humans. He had lived with a boy, and he had loved that boy and had learned the humans' ways, and their ways had been his ways for most of his life. He crept closer to watch this group from a stand of bushes.

They were gathered around a fire. Although there were women and youths in the group, they all wore the clothes of the war-sick men he remembered from a year before. A truck pulled in, and Pax recognized that also — large and green and smelling of burnt metal and oil.

He made his way back to where his family waited.

Human war-sick have come. Full knowledge passed between Pax and his mate: where the war-sick were, the earth could blow without warning, the air itself could shatter. Foxes could lose legs. Foxes could be killed.

Their home at the Deserted Farm was no longer safe.

Bristle looked back at her kits. *We must move our family.*

Pax shared this understanding also. Bristle couldn't leave, so he would go out to find his family a new home. *But not tonight. Tonight we teach them to drink.*

Bristle and Pax slipped down to a place on the gravelly shore where it would be safe. They bent to the quiet water and showed the kits how to lap it with their tongues.

The kits bounced down the bank. They batted at the surface of the water and jumped back at its startling liquidity. They pranced in and out, they splashed along the edge, they dunked each other.

Bristle and Pax stepped back to watch, Bristle keeping a wary eye on the other side of the reservoir, where the humans were.

Pax noticed that the kits were changing. Their gray coats were becoming redder each day, and fresh points of white fur tipped their tails and cheeks. Their legs had darkened and lengthened. They were strong enough now to knock each other over.

After a few minutes, all three settled down and learned the new task of drinking.

Excited by their accomplishment, thirsty from the long journey, they drank and they drank and they drank.

10

"He won't come."

Vola didn't even look up from the biscuit dough she was rolling out. "He will come."

"He never does."

"Well, he will this time. His only grandson is leaving in the morning, be gone for a month. Slice those carrots, then set the table. For *three*."

Peter picked up a knife and put a carrot onto the cutting board. "What makes you so sure?"

Vola sprinkled flour over the slab of dough. "All right. Because I didn't *invite* him this time. I *told* him that dinner is at six thirty."

That thought worried him more. "He's not the kind of person who likes being told what to do," he warned.

Vola shrugged. She began cutting out biscuits with a glass. "Maybe he is angry that you chose to live here instead of with him, but you are still his only grandson, his only family, eh? You are leaving, and so he will come."

Peter hoped she was right, but only because she had gone to so much trouble. A duck roasting in the oven was stuffed with hickory nuts and spring onions. Yesterday, she'd dug up the last of the potatoes and picked the first of the peas. She'd sent Peter out early this morning to gather watercress from the stream for a salad, and when he'd returned, he'd found her making a peach pie.

That pie sat on the windowsill now. All day he'd smelled it, even down at his own cabin when he'd been nailing the last shingles, its fragrant steam curling along the path like the beckoning fingers of a cartoon pie.

He wondered if Vola remembered that peaches were the first thing he'd eaten when he'd landed here a year ago, starving and broken-boned. He'd wolfed down a whole jar, and later that first day she had told him a story about herself, about how as a little girl she used to sneak out to the orchard at night, stack a pile of peaches on her belly, and eat them in the moonlight.

When the fruit ripened last summer, he'd tried the same thing himself. He'd snuck out at midnight — there was no moon, but a million fireflies glittered — and eaten those soft peaches until his face was sticky with juice.

That night, for the first time since giving up Pax, he had let his tears flow — his face all juice-wet in the dark anyway. When he'd crept back inside, Vola was up. He saw from her expression that she knew he'd been crying, but she left him alone about it.

Now that peach pie was about killing him with all that it said about this place he was leaving, about this person he had hurt because she'd invited him to stay for good. He turned his back on that pie. "You're wrong. He won't come," he said again. "We'll have to go over there tomorrow morning, get my permission signed."

"He'll come," Vola said. She slid the tray of biscuits into the oven, closed the oven door firmly as if that was that.

And she was right. Just fifteen minutes later, he heard the chug and sigh of the old man's Chevy pulling in beside Vola's truck. He ran to the window to be sure, then swept a quick look around the cabin.

A fire blazed and all the oil lamps were lit, burnishing the furniture to gold. The floor was freshly waxed, the table had been scrubbed and was set with her good china, a fat bunch of daffodils sprang out of a yellow jug on the mantel. Through the windows, the hills glowed blue in the dusk.

He got up to open the door and watched as his grandfather made a show of cracking his back, and then looked around, taking in the place. Peter swelled a little, thinking of how it would look to him: the orchard in pale bloom, the vegetable garden with its neat rows of bright green against the red soil, and just beyond the solid barn, his own new cabin.

When he began to pick his way up the stone path, Peter saw that his grandfather's hair was combed into neat strands over

his forehead and his face was pink — he'd gone home after work, showered and shaved fresh.

"You came," Peter called, stupidly. "I'm glad."

"Can't stay too late," his grandfather grumbled. "Some of us go to a job." He stopped on the granite slab of a doorstep and looked inside with the same surprise Peter himself had felt the first day he'd come, as if he'd expected the inside to match the outside, rough and primitive.

"Come in, come in," Vola encouraged from the kitchen. "I hope you are hungry."

Peter knew he would be. The old man usually opened up a bag of chips and a beer the instant he got home from work, then heated up a supper out of cans. Tonight Vola's home smelled like a restaurant.

Vola set the food on the table right away, and filled their plates until the gravy ran off the sides. She made small talk while the old man ate — nothing but weather, the good grades Peter was earning, and how he'd made the baseball team. Peter's grandfather mostly just nodded as he chewed.

Then Vola piled a fresh round of everything onto their plates. "So," she said. "Tomorrow."

Peter put down his fork.

"I'll drive him," she went on. "Your grandson made me buy that truck, I might as well use it. I'll drop him at that reservoir in Landsburg. He'll travel the rest of the way with the platoon."

"Platoon, Water Warriors." The old man swept a hand dismissively. "No right to use those terms, not real military."

"Why aren't they?" Vola asked mildly.

"I served, my father served, the boy's father served," he said. "Real military is . . ." He raised his fists and bunched them.

"Vola served, too," Peter said.

The old man glanced down at Vola's leg. "Right, right," he conceded. "You know what I mean. Warriors are . . . it's about power. Not a bunch of do-gooders."

"Well, that is not what I believe." Vola said it in a completely neutral voice. No challenge, no judgment on someone who believed something else.

Peter had come to appreciate Vola's technique. It defused things, let the other person hold a different side without asking for a fight. Still, he felt his belly muscles tighten in a way they hadn't in a year.

But then Vola picked up the pitcher of cider and refilled the glasses. Before she set the pitcher back, she held it up. "This was a gift," she said, and Peter relaxed. She was moving away from the subject. "It was made from the clay around here. A local craftsman. I had given him some firewood when he ran out."

Peter's grandfather grunted in appreciation.

"How many years did it take him to learn the trade, I wonder," Vola mused. "How many hours to create this piece? How many times has it been useful, filling our cups?"

Peter picked up his fork as his grandfather bent to his food.

But Vola wasn't finished. "Now think of it: I throw this pitcher against the wall. That is a lot of power I show. But anyone can break something. The power I respect is in the making." She set the pitcher down. She turned to Peter and lifted her glass. "And maybe most of all, I respect anyone who chooses to *rebuild* something."

Peter's grandfather stopped chewing. He nodded grudgingly.

And then Vola offered him some grace. "Besides, Peter will be learning useful skills. Pipelayers are princes these days, well diggers are kings. That is not likely to change anytime soon."

"Never hurts to know an honest trade," the old man mumbled his agreement, saving face. He fumbled with his napkin and a spoon clattered to the floor.

Peter tipped back in his chair to reach into the silverware drawer behind him. Without looking, he pulled out a new spoon and placed it beside his grandfather's plate.

The old man took it, but he looked as if he'd been struck. And then Peter realized what his grandfather had seen: his own grandson so comfortable in this place that he didn't have to look to retrieve a spoon.

This isn't my home, he wanted to say. "I need a permission slip to stay at the camps," he said instead. "Signed by a family member. You're my family."

And it worked. Peter saw his grandfather's face soften with relief and maybe even a little pride. He patted his pockets for a pen and signed the note with a flourish.

They took their pie out on the porch and Peter lit the lanterns. As they ate, feet up on the railing, watching a slender crescent moon rise, his grandfather became talkative. He warned Peter of dangers from his own time in the service, and of mistakes he should avoid, all in a protective way that surprised Peter.

He didn't think advice from two generations ago would be relevant, but he let his grandfather talk anyway, kind of in shock. His grandfather was acting like . . . well, like a grandfather.

"You stay safe, boy," he said at the end. He got up, thanked Vola for the meal, and shook Peter's hand.

After they waved him off, Vola said, "He will come more often now, I think."

Peter moved away without answering. He collected the empty plates and balanced the half-eaten pie on top.

Vola followed him inside. "You know, he is getting older, Peter. And someday, if you want . . ." She gestured out the window toward his cabin, toward the land beyond the orchard.

"Stop." Peter suddenly knew what she was going to say. That there would come a time when his grandfather would need some help. That Peter could take him in, build him a place here. And he knew what would happen if she said that. He would start imagining feeling comfortable and safe and part of a family. He would let his guard down.

And that he could never do again.

He suddenly realized that everything here — Vola, the cabin he was building, the town he was coming to know, his grandfather, Ben and the others — everything here was too dangerous.

A month away would not solve this. The solution was obvious. He would not come back.

After he served with the Warriors, he would move into his old house. Alone. Safe. And he wouldn't come back.

He went to the back porch and grabbed his sleeping bag. When he came through the kitchen, Vola was wrapping leftovers.

"I'm going to sleep at my cabin tonight," he said.

Vola nodded as if she'd expected it. She handed him a wedge of pie, wrapped in wax paper. "In case you wake up hungry."

Peter left, and as soon as he passed the barn, he flung the pie into a patch of weeds.

It was time.

Pax stretched and ruffled his fur in the late afternoon sunshine. The wind was from the south; it would mask his approach and also warn him of any dangers ahead. There would be no moon, offering him cover of darkness. He had cached two ducks the night before and there were still potatoes in the field and fat mice in the barn, so Bristle and the kits would not go hungry in his absence.

He refreshed his scent markings to warn off any territory challenge while he was away and then visited the den. The kits were awake and nursing. They had grown so much that Bristle had to stretch out to accommodate them. In a few minutes, Pax knew, they would scramble outside, and it would be all she could do to keep them herded together and out of trouble.

He pressed his cheek against Bristle's. *I will leave now.*

He nuzzled each of his kits, reassuring them he would return and ordering them to obey their mother. The kits raised milky noses to kiss their father's cheek. Then the two males went back to their meals.

But the little vixen wriggled out between her brothers and followed her father to the entrance.

No. Stay. I will return. Pax left, but before he rounded the shed corner he looked back. His daughter stood beside the steps, blinking in the low sun rays. Her coat, the brightest of the kits', glowed nearly as red as her mother's. She pricked her ears to him and trotted out.

Pax ran back, picked her up by the loose skin of her neck, and carried her into the den. Bristle cuffed her daughter to her belly and held her with a firm paw, and Pax slipped out again.

This time, he did not look back.

72

He loped through the fields of the deserted farms, and then entered the forest. He ran silently between the trees on pine-needled deer paths, and even when full darkness fell, broken only by thin starshine, he moved easily. The trail was familiar — a year ago, he and Bristle and Runt had made this same journey in reverse, leaving the Broad Valley that had been Bristle's home.

Pax had first seen the Broad Valley soon after being abandoned by his boy. He'd been waiting for Peter to come and rescue him, because he had not yet learned that he did not need to be rescued. In those few days, filled with fear and worry but also the exhilaration of new freedom, he

had appreciated the valley's bounty and advantageous location. Pax might have stayed and made a home, but the need to find his boy had urged him south.

He had traveled with Gray, the old fox from the Broad Valley, to a place where a river fell and then flattened out beside an old stone mill. It was there the war-sick humans had come, and there that Gray had died. Bristle and Runt had followed Pax, and it was there that the humans blew up the earth, which tore Runt's leg from his body and burned Bristle's full tail to a blackened whip.

And it was there that Pax's boy had come back.

That day, two coyotes had followed Runt's blood trail to the clearing above the humans' camp. The coyotes had Bristle treed, and it would not be long before they dragged Runt from his hiding place. Pax was tiring from fending them off when he'd heard his boy's voice from the camp below. He'd barked for help, and Peter had come. His boy had chased off the coyotes.

Pax had felt a great relief and joy at the reunion with Peter, and he knew that Peter felt that also.

But Pax was confused. Peter sometimes carried a strange grief-yearning, and that day it was as strong as his joy.

When he pulled out a familiar toy, Pax became wary. *Retrieve the toy and bark*, the old game used to promise, *and Peter will join you* — but Pax now knew that the promise was a lie.

Peter threw the toy.

Pax hesitated, trying to sort the *go-stay* puzzle. When Peter had turned away, Pax understood that his boy wanted to separate from him, and so he had bounded into the thicket after the toy.

But he had not picked it up and barked. Instead, he crept back out.

He'd seen his boy hurry to the far edge of the clearing, hopping awkwardly with an injured leg.

Pax had followed and watched from the tree line as Peter stumbled down the hill, falling twice in his hurry, and met his father. They had embraced for a long time, then entered a tent together.

And then Pax had turned and joined Bristle and Runt and formed a family.

That afternoon, the three foxes had taken shelter in a warren of groundhog burrows too narrow for coyotes to enter. They rested there safely for many days. Runt grew stronger and learned to move well on three legs. Bristle bit at the crusted fur of her ruined brush, breaking it open time and again to clean it.

At last, when Runt could sprint for short bursts and Bristle's tail had stopped weeping, Bristle grew restless to move farther from the humans and their war, and so they returned to the Broad Valley.

There, Gray's mate had welcomed them. She had given birth to a litter of six kits, and Pax and Bristle hunted for her. They would have been welcome to make their home there, but the human war grew closer and so Pax led his new family farther north, through two more highland forests separated by two more valleys — one shallow, and the other steep and rocky — until they had come to the Deserted Farm.

It was the shallow valley Pax now entered. At the bottom, a creek glinted in the pale starlight. As the sky lightened with dawn, he crossed it, and then began the climb up the next ridge.

He reached the peak as the sun rose over the pines to the east, and Pax began looking for a safe spot to sleep for a few hours. He was just settling down in a springy bed of club moss, when a new scent curled up through the trees.

Fire.

Sitting on the wide reservoir wall with his legs dangling through the railing's steel bars, Peter felt a thrill run through him. From now on, he was on his own. Tonight, this moment, his new life was beginning.

He'd felt this way once before. At seven years old, he'd realized that nothing would ever be the same after his mother died, and he'd been right. But this time the turning point was different. This time he was choosing it.

It was different also because his future looked better, not grimmer. His future looked like the reservoir before him — broad and deep and full of secret promise. And it looked like the outpost behind him, offering what he needed: food, clothing, shelter, and important things to do, with people only as close as he allowed them.

He felt safe here, from the moment the operations sergeant had shaken his hand in welcome a few hours ago.

The ride itself had been hard. He'd decided not to tell Vola that he wasn't coming back, to instead write a letter when he moved into his old house. A cowardice or a kindness, he didn't know.

Over and over, he'd glanced at her and realized he'd never see her again, and he'd almost changed his mind, but he hadn't broken. Once, she'd said, "I may not feel like family to you, Peter, but you feel like mine. You cannot change that, so you may as well accept it, eh?" and he'd felt his throat swell. He hadn't answered and that felt like a lie. When they'd pulled into the outpost, she'd advised him again, "Fill your cup whenever you can," and this time he'd understood that she wasn't talking about water and his eyes had stung, but he'd gotten himself under control and opened the truck door.

And then she was gone. As he'd walked to the intake tent, it had seemed as if gravity wasn't working quite right.

He'd done the camp orientation in a mild daze: a tour of the barracks and the work sites and a film about the mission. He'd been given a guidebook about company responsibilities. Everyone did some cleaning and food prep, and tomorrow he was supposed to choose a work unit. Infrastructure, Communications, Ecosystems — one of those.

Now, having eaten and stowed his gear under a cot at the end of a row, his only job was to "get to know the other Junior Warriors," as the sergeant had suggested. It hadn't been an order, though.

Peter peered down at the dark water through the railing and listened to the murmur of voices behind him, brightened once in a while by laughter. Just then, he caught the surprising scent of burnt sugar.

He shifted to observe the people gathered around the fire — troops, he was supposed to call them. Most were wearing leftover combat gear. They were evenly divided, men and women, and a variety of ages. Peter saw the three other Junior Warriors sitting together, tossing something between them. Two people — two *troops* — caught his eye. A boy and a girl,

maybe nineteen or twenty, and something about the way they were sitting made him think they were a couple.

Peter smelled the hot sugar again. His mouth watered.

He got up. He walked along the wall and then down the steps to the ground. There, he debated a moment and then decided: he would join the circle, but not talk.

He chose a log next to the one the girl and boy sat on, because he saw now that they were definitely a couple, the boy's hand resting on the girl's knee. A couple would be more likely to ignore him.

The girl wore a flowered scarf knotted around thick, dark curls. She smiled at Peter when he dropped down.

The boy beside her leaned forward — his head looked freshly shaved, and Peter saw a tattoo on his neck — and tipped his hand, then turned back to the fire.

The girl handed Peter a bag of marshmallows and the stick she'd been holding. "They were a gift," she said. "People are so generous wherever we go. They're so grateful for getting their water back. An old woman from the last town gave them to us, since Samuel and I are always camping out."

The boy, Samuel, leaned back out again. "Jade and I are the advance reconnaissance team," he told Peter. "The woman said her grandson was in the war, and marshmallows were what he had missed most."

"People try to give you all kinds of things," Jade added. "Jewelry, mementos of their families who were lost in the war. We can't take anything, except for the food."

A man began telling about someone trying to give him a horse. Then a woman across the circle began a story about opossums getting in the mess tent, and people started laughing, and Peter let his mind wander, watching his marshmallow cook.

He ate it when it was perfect — crunchy outside, but dripping sticky-sweet inside. He thought again that he liked how his future looked. He could live like this just fine.

But then the girl, Jade, ruined everything. "We saw a family of foxes last week."

Peter stiffened.

"Parents and three little kits," she went on. "They were so cute."

Peter wiped his hands on his jeans and balanced the stick on a rock beside him. "What did they look like? The parents, I mean?" he asked, hoping no one caught the tremble in his voice.

"What did they look like?" Samuel repeated. He licked marshmallow off his fingers. "Don't they all look the same?"

"Sure, right." Peter drew his knees up and hugged them to his chest. He shouldn't have asked.

"No, Samuel," the girl said. She turned to Peter. "They were across the reservoir, so we were watching through binoculars. But I remember something. One adult had a weird tail. Not fluffy. Like a whip. As if the fur had been stripped off."

Peter's heart quickened. The last time he'd seen Pax, his fox was with a vixen. She had a sharp little face and bright copper fur, but a tail that looked as if it had been burnt. "The other adult," he asked, trying not to sound eager. "Do you remember what it looked like?"

"Sorry," Jade said, and it sounded like she meant it. "I was paying attention to those kits. It was obvious they'd never seen water before, and I thought, What would it be like to encounter water for the first time?" She turned her gaze to the reservoir, shimmering under the stars. "Water. Magic, right?"

The people in the circle had quieted. They were all listening to Jade now.

"And then they got into it. They were exactly like us — like human kids, you know? First they seemed scared of the water, but then their curiosity got them and they started sniffing it, dipping in their paws, jumping back. Pretty soon they were horsing around, splashing in it, knocking each other over. And then they settled down to drink, and I thought, I'm glad it's their first time here. Because it's pretty clean now."

84

"Pretty clean?" Peter asked.

"Clean enough that it won't kill them. We've gotten out the toxins. All that's left now is to reestablish a biome."

She pointed at the bag of marshmallows. Peter shook his head. He couldn't swallow anything right now.

"It was funny," Jade went on, twisting a corner of her scarf. "Samuel and I have been doing this for four months now. It's always the same: we come into a place where the water's ruined, we clean it up, move downstream. Repeat. You know that besides the people moving back, it means the animals in the area will survive afterward, and that's great, of course. But this is the first time I actually *felt* it, that it became *real,* what we're doing. Because of that fox family. I felt like now those fox kits are *mine*."

"As if you could own a fox," Samuel scoffed.

"I had one once," Peter said quietly. He waited for the pain to clutch his throat, tight as a pair of hands. When it subsided, he said, "I didn't own him, though, that's not the right word." He knew the right word — love, he had loved Pax and Pax

85

had loved him — but he didn't say that word. "He was tame."

On both sides of him, others joined in, talking about pets they'd had, moving on.

But Peter didn't move on.

They were only fifty miles north of where he'd last left Pax, and fifty miles was nothing for a fox. And how many other foxes had scarred tails? What if it *was* that vixen and Pax these two had seen? If so, he had a litter of kits now.

Peter couldn't help thinking about Pax as a kit. He recalled the moment he'd lifted the ball of fur out of the den. He remembered the fox's heartbeat, fast but strong enough that he could feel it through the fleece of his sweatshirt against the skin of his own belly.

He lifted his gaze to the dark woods beside him, and his own heart quickened: it really could have been his fox the couple had seen. Pax and his family could be living here.

He slumped back. Now, every minute he'd be thinking about his pet. Now, every time he saw a movement in the woods, a flash of orange, his heart would lift and then it would crash. He would run the penance a hundred times a day, and it would never work.

"When are we leaving?" he interrupted Jade and Samuel, who were talking together.

Samuel shrugged. "Most of the company will finish here in a week, maybe ten days."

A week, maybe ten days, was too long.

"Some will stay on to reseed the reservoir. Fish, shellfish, aquatic plants," Jade added. "That's usually another week, so two weeks from now."

Two weeks would kill him. "You said you're the reconnaissance team, you go first. When are you leaving?"

"Tomorrow," Samuel said. "But —"

"I'll come with you. I'll sign up for your team."

"No, you can't," Jade said. "We don't take Juniors. We're roughing it."

"I've lived in a cabin without electricity for the last year. I can cook over a fire, use a compass, build a solar still. Everything."

Jade hesitated for a moment, but then she shook her head. "No. Living in a cabin is one thing, but the place we're going? It's in some pretty rugged territory. It takes special skills, and we have to travel light."

"But I need to go!" Peter stood up, folded his arms across his chest. "Please. I know that territory. I'm from there. I made a trip there last year. Starting at the cliffs in the west, through the woods, forty miles to that old mill by the falls on the river where the troops were stationed, all alone and —"

"No, Jade and I don't take Juniors," Samuel said firmly.

"Alone and *on crutches*."

Samuel and Jade both looked up at him. "On crutches?" Samuel asked.

"I broke my foot. I trekked forty miles, I made camp, I scaled those cliffs, I forded that river, *on crutches*."

Samuel raised his hands in surrender. Jade grinned. "Get some sleep," she said. "We leave at dawn."

At the crest of the ridge, Pax looked down over the fire a quarter mile below.

Flames sizzled along the edges of a blackened oval at the valley's basin. The fire consumed the grasses with a soft hissing, not the crackling roar of a monster on the loose, but its smoke was choking. After a moment Pax heard a man's shout and another's reply. He had not scented the humans through the smoke, but he was not surprised they were there — humans were often involved in fire.

Pax winced and drew closer, until he could make out two men, and then two more at the far edge of the blaze. And he was relieved. For all its power, fire served humans, and humans could stop it at will. He had often watched his own boy kill fire by drowning it in a stream of water.

The humans would stop the fire soon; they always did. If they sent it up the hill, he would leave along the ridge to seek out the river, where he knew the fire could not follow. But now he would rest and eat.

He made his way back up the hill where the air was clearer. He clawed the bark from a fallen pitch pine and made a meal of grubs. Then he took cover in the tree's boughs, still dense with browning needles, backing in until only his face protruded. He would rest here until the fire was out, then continue south again.

Pax rested without sleeping until mid-afternoon. When he looked out, he saw that the humans had moved along to the west, their fire moving with them. Directly below him now he saw only flickering sparks on the scorched ground. Belly low, he crept down the slope.

As he moved onto the blackened fringe, the ground grew warmer. Here and there, woody shrubs still glowed. The air smelled of burnt grasses and seared dirt. There was the scent of roasted flesh also, and he came upon many burnt mice. He ignored those, but when he found a clutch of partridge eggs in a hollow that the fire had barely singed, he ate them. The insides were warm and surprisingly solid, not wet.

He ventured farther toward the center of the basin. The ground there was hotter. A dried seedpod exploded with a pop just in front of him, and Pax jumped. Darting away, he burned a back paw on a smoldering branch.

Pax hurried back up the slope, hid himself behind the pitch-pine trunk, and licked the paw. He curled his brush around his snout to keep out the smoke and closed his eyes. He would try to cross again in the cool of dusk.

This time, before starting out, he climbed to the spine of the ridge to scan for any danger that might have followed him. He expected none — when he'd traveled through the night before, he'd found no sign of any predators at all — but until his paw healed, he would not be as quick as usual. He would have to be more cautious.

The air on this back side of the ridge was clear. The low sun's light fell upon the birches on the far slope like slanting rain:

drenching their canopies, flowing down the branches, and dripping from the bright leaves. A cloud of pale blue butterflies rose and fell like breath.

For several moments Pax saw nothing that alarmed him. He licked his injured paw again and was about to leave, when he caught a slight trembling in the shrubs below the birches. He stilled.

He followed the movement down into the meadow. He could see nothing but the path of ruffled grasses, so the intruder was too small to be a threat. A rabbit, perhaps, more careless than usual, or a clumsy skunk out for its evening hunt.

At a bare patch of gravel that Pax himself had passed, the creature emerged.

And Pax sprang up, charged with sudden fear and joy in equal measure. He bounded down the hill at a full run, skimmed the creek at the bottom, and reached his daughter, panting.

As he drew up, the kit stopped. She sat down and lifted her head, as though expecting to be greeted. *You left us.*

Pax checked the tiny fox all over. She was dusty and her heart was beating fast, but she was unharmed. He rose to his full height, pricked his ears forward, and straightened his tail. *You should not have followed me.* He reminded her that she had been ordered to stay behind, to obey her mother.

The kit flattened herself in front of her father. *You went far.* She laid her chin on his paw.

Pax warned her of the dangers a small young fox traveling alone could encounter, which were many. He admonished her for her disobedience. Throughout his chastening, the kit remained obediently still.

At last Pax crouched low, so that she would know she was forgiven. Her eyes were closed and when he licked her cheek, she let out a snore and rolled over.

Pax picked up his sleeping daughter. Although she swung from his jaws as he bounded back up to the ridge, she did not wake. He tucked her in the crooked elbow of a branch at the fallen pitch pine, and she didn't stir. Even when he settled himself around her, his chin on her small skull, she only purred in her sleep.

Pax curled his brush over her. When she had rested, he would return her to Bristle in the den. He would order her to stay and he would be sterner. But now, he had only to keep her safe.

14

The first day, they covered only six miles, but they were six hard miles: scrabbling through greenbrier and clambering up and down swales, fording the river whenever the land got impassable on one side or the other, all carrying their heavy packs.

In addition to his own clothes and camping gear, Peter's backpack contained the cardboard box with his father's ashes. As they hiked, the box thumped his back with each step, and Peter imagined it as a reassuring pat.

Up at dawn, they'd tramped for four hours straight, making their way to the first testing point. The river tumbled along next to them as if in a hurry, too loud for easy conversation. Tough terrain like that, nobody had the energy to talk much anyway, which suited Peter fine. He'd learned a lot about his two companions, though.

He'd noticed that Jade was quicker on her feet than either he or Samuel, hopping nimbly over obstacles and humming under her breath, as if it was a game to her. She paused often, and Peter learned to follow her gaze because it always led to something he wouldn't want to have missed: an oriole so bright against the dark forest that its feathers seemed flames; a spiderweb jeweled with river mist; pink toadstools that looked like they'd sprouted straight out of a fairy tale. Samuel, though, plowed a straight, head-down path forward, like a machine.

Once Peter had grabbed his arm. "Careful. I broke my foot in a place just like this," he'd said, pointing to a muddy passage. "You can't see the roots under the mud, and they're slippery." He'd pulled out his rain poncho and spread it over the patch. "We'll use this. It'll be safer. I can wash it off on the river tonight."

At the first collection point, they set up a camp table and arranged the equipment.

Samuel was explaining how to label samples when Peter stood up. "I smell smoke."

Jade nodded. "It's another Water Warriors crew. All along the valleys, where the creeks have been contaminated, they're setting fire to the invasive weeds that have taken over. Then they'll reseed with native grasses."

It felt good to know there were other crews out besides them, making things right after the war. Peter felt part of something large and important.

Then they'd drawn straws for the three jobs: river water, feeder streams, sediment. After the collecting, they'd eaten a quick lunch of sandwiches, packed up the table and the gear, and set out again.

After making their way downhill for a while, they'd all suddenly drawn up short. A rockslide had made the bank on their side too unstable to cross.

"The test equipment can't get wet." Samuel looked down in dismay at the river, narrow and deep there, its waters falling angrily over the spilled rocks. "Can't risk it. We'll have to backtrack."

"Or . . . wait." Peter looked around until he saw what he was hoping for.

"What are you smiling about?" Jade asked him.

Peter walked to a cluster of white-trunked trees beside the river, then began to shimmy up the tallest. "Birch-bending," he called down when he was near the top. Then he grabbed the smooth trunk with both hands and lowered his body. The tree bent down and down, arcing over the river and depositing him on the other side gently.

He let go and it snapped back up straight.

Jade held her arms up high and clapped her appreciation. Then she tightened her pack straps and edged up the tree. The birch eased her down lightly, as though it knew it was carrying something special. When it was his turn, Samuel couldn't hide a grin as he scrambled up the tree and swung across, and it made him look suddenly like a boy of Peter's own age.

And something changed. For the rest of the hike, Peter felt he wasn't following the two Water Warriors like an eager puppy, wasn't in their way, wasn't part of their duty. He felt he was one of them, and they made their way as equals.

When they arrived at the second testing location, they'd taken their samples, logged the data, and then set a fire with the deadwood Peter chopped up. Soon, stew was bubbling over the flames.

Peter sat on a rock with his back to the fire, watching dusk fall over the river. Above the tree line, a star came out, and then another and another. The air smelled smoky, but also mossy and full of secrets. Peter's whole body ached with exhaustion, but he felt sharply alert. He felt part of the night.

Samuel scooped stew into three bowls and passed them out along with spoons. Peter turned into the circle. Jade handed him a piece of bread. He watched her fold hers in half and dip it into the hot stew, and he did the same.

"Easier going tomorrow," Samuel said after a while. He got up and gathered the bowls and spoons. "Eight miles at least, maybe ten. By the way, that was something today. Birch-bending. Good job, man."

And Peter was glad for the dark, because he felt himself blush. He got up and spread his bedroll across from where the couple had theirs and climbed in. And let himself hear it again. *Good job, man.* The compliment meant even more coming from Samuel, who seemed to think of words as coins and was careful about spending any. He wished his grandfather could have heard it. His father.

Peter pressed his fingertip to his throat and felt the new hard bulge of his larynx. Last summer, the unpredictability of his changing voice had been embarrassing, but now he liked that his voice sounded tougher. He liked what it meant: that he was closer to being a man.

And in fact, he'd been firming up all over this year. His palms had calloused and his shoulders had grown solid from the month he'd been on crutches last spring. His back had broadened from a summer farming Vola's fields; his arms and legs grown strong from the six months he'd spent building his cabin.

And when he ran his penance, sometimes it even felt as if the center of his heart was hardening up. As if he'd swallowed a pebble and it had lodged in the core of the beating muscle.

But he would need to toughen up even more to make it, living on his own.

Peter pushed a fist against his chest, imagining there really was a stone in his heart. And thought, *Make it a rock.*

15

At the sound of human voices, Pax awoke, instantly alert.

His daughter was curled between his forelegs. He extricated himself without waking her and crept out to peer down into the valley. The midmorning sun shone on the burned meadow. No breeze stirred and there was no sign of the humans, but he heard their voices again.

He climbed up to the top of the ridge to look back north. Below, the same men were back, huddled together at the creek in their bright green vests. They lifted chunky cans and Pax watched as they spread apart, two on each side of the creek. They bent to the grass, igniting small flames and then walked west, lighting more along the way. The fires crackled and jumped into rolling carpets on either side of the creek, cutting Pax and his daughter off from their route home.

Pax hurried back and woke the kit. He led her to the top of the ridge and crouched low with her. *Fire. Learn the scent.*

The little vixen sniffed. She squeezed her eyes against the curls of smoke.

Run from it. Fire is always hungry, even when it is human-tamed, like this one.

The kit's gaze swept the valley, then her eyes widened. *Those are humans?*

Pax saw her surprise at the brightness of their coats. *They have no need to conceal themselves. They are not prey. But humans are not always green.* He remembered how Peter would add or peel off layers all day. *You cannot know them by their color. They shed their skins at will.*

His daughter shrank back under his legs. *Dangerous.*

Pax looked down at the men, standing together now, watching over their fire. In the year that he had been living free, he had met no other fox who had loved a human as he had. But he had learned that most were comfortable living alongside them. Bristle's terror of them was unusual, but it was fair — she had lost her parents and a sister to humans; she had lost her bushy tail; her brother had lost his leg to them at the Broken Hill.

Bristle would teach her kits what she'd learned.

Dangerous, he confirmed. *Stay away. We must leave now. We cannot retrace our trail back. To the east, a river flows. We will cross to it by the ridge, then follow that river back home.*

River?

Endless water, rushing like a great wind. Its path leads from the reservoir south to the Broad Valley and beyond. We will meet that river and then follow it upstream to the reservoir and we will be safe from the fire because fire will not cross water.

Pax was certain of this. At the place where the war-sick humans blew up the earth, the flames had stopped at the river every time. *Water always defeats fire, and so fire respects its territory.*

At first the kit kept up with Pax's easy trot, scurrying behind him on her short legs. But she had to clamber over the rocks, fallen branches, hillocks of grass that Pax cleared without pausing, and over and over, she stopped to sniff at anything that might be food.

When Pax caught the scent of a rabbit warren, he ordered her to stay hidden and motionless while he caught a meal. He dropped the rabbit in front of the kit. But she only nosed it, then looked up, expectant.

Pax remembered how Bristle fed the kits, and he chewed the soft belly meat and offered it back, as he had seen her do. The kit gulped the food until her sides bulged.

They set out again, their pace slower this time. As the sun set, the little fox began to stumble in her exhaustion.

Three times Pax attempted to pick her up by the fur of her neck to carry her across a rough patch, and each time she yowled her indignation, squirming until he let her down. By the time the crescent moon rose, she was staggering.

Pax felt tired himself. He looked over the ridge for a less exposed place to rest. At the base of a short cliff, he saw a flat basin of scrub.

They angled their way down, both of them sliding on the scree of shale and flint. At the bottom, Pax found a niche in the cliff.

The spot was well protected: if any intruder entered from above, a cascade of sediment would wake them; if any came from the front, the dried stems of the underbrush would rattle. He smelled neither prey nor predators — in fact, no animal life at all. Still, he felt anxious.

He circled around in the hollow and settled down. The kit curled up beside him, closed her eyes, and fluffed her tail over her little pointed face. Pax waited until he was sure she was asleep and then set out to patrol the area for dangers he could not scent.

Nothing stirred in the scrub. More surprisingly, there were no fresh trails — not the broken twigs of deer, not the trampled paths of raccoon, not even the underbrush tunnels of rodents.

Past the scrub was a row of tall bare pines. Slices of dark pond glinted between their silver trunks.

Pax sniffed. The water smelled strangely of metal, like the inside of his boy's car. He could scent none of the things that usually grew in, or around, ponds. He crept to the shore. The pond was a perfect oval of blackness so still that each star was reflected on its surface. Nothing moved along its edges, which were littered with bleached bones.

He relaxed. There was no danger here.

He drank and then slipped back to the hollow in the cliff wall and curled himself around his daughter. She did not wake, but she coughed in her sleep. In the dry cough, Pax heard a need for water.

When she woke, he would lead her to the still, safe pond.

16

After a meal of soup and biscuits, Peter
and Jade had claimed rocks overlooking
the river, a lantern between them. Samuel
leaned against a wide tree trunk beside
them, reading with a flashlight.

"Nine miles today," Peter said. He'd
kept track of them and felt a physical relief
around noon when he figured they'd gone
far enough that he wouldn't risk running
into Pax anymore.

Beside him, Jade groaned. "Only nine
miles. I always wish it were more. There's
so much to do. Although it's not as if we
can hurry it along."

"The water samples we took today and yesterday," Peter said. "Could you tell anything from them yet?"

"Some. We'll have to wait for the lab reports to know for sure, but I can already see a difference."

"A difference?"

"Samuel and I tested this same stretch before we set up at the reservoir. Now that the water's pure there, yes, this part of the river is noticeably cleaner. It will get worse as we go downstream, as it picks up water from contaminated feeder streams. And then once we're at the next cleanup site, it will be really bad again. It was a military camp at an old mill. A ton of bad stuff was used there. It's leaking out."

Peter turned back to the river. He and his father had talked about a lot of things the last day at the mill site, but Peter hadn't asked him what exactly his job was in the military. He hadn't wanted to know. Now, he couldn't help wondering if he'd had a part in contaminating that water. "Is that place the worst around here?"

Jade sighed. "The worst? It's bad, but no. There's a pond. It's just a mile west from one of our collection sites." She called over to Samuel. "Remember Oval Pond? What is it — two days away?"

"Two, maybe three," Samuel answered without lifting his eyes from his book.

"Oval Pond. It used to be teeming with life, a little gem. But the Resistance dumped in a bunch of heavy metals after they blew up the bridge, and now nothing lives in it. Nothing. The vegetation all around it died, too, even the old trees. It's silent there. Dead."

Beside Peter, bats swooped over the river, peepers chirped from their secret trees, and an owl hooted softly. Life everywhere. "There are no animals there?"

Jade shook her head. "The young all die, and the adults move on."

"Just the young die?"

"Their nervous systems are still developing. They drink the contaminated water and it damages them in ways they can't recover from."

"Not that Jade didn't try," Samuel called from his reading.

Jade dropped her head. "Not anymore," she murmured. "I won't anymore."

111

"She did, though." Samuel closed his book and put it in his pack. He came over and sat beside Jade and put his arm around her, a look of pride on his face.

Jade sighed again. "We found a nest of raccoons near that pond a month ago. Two little cubs dead, two really sick. I figured it was lead poisoning from the way they were wobbling around. I wanted to save them."

Peter could relate to that. When he'd found Pax so near death, he'd felt an overwhelming desire to do something, anything, to save the kit. He felt a rush of sympathy for this girl. "What did you do?"

Jade lifted her shoulders in a tiny shrug. "Milk, activated charcoal. Tried to flush the toxins out of them."

"Did it work?"

"Don't know. The parents allowed me to handle the cubs and they stuck around, so at least they weren't going to give them up. But the company arrived at the reservoir and we had to leave. Duty calls, right?"

"Will we go there?" Peter asked. "Will we take samples from that pond? Maybe you'll see them again."

"No," Samuel said. "It's a kettle pond."

"It's groundwater fed," Jade explained. "Our mission is strictly the reservoir and the river. So that pond is another company's mission. We just happened to run into it while we were waiting for the company to arrive." She stretched out to rest her chin on her knees. "Besides, right now I get to imagine that those baby raccoons are okay, that they got better and they're running around doing normal raccoon things. It would be too hard to learn they hadn't."

Peter saw from her face just how hard it would be. "You must see a lot of bad stuff like that doing this work. Why did you sign up?" he asked.

Jade raised her palms, incredulous at the question. "Water! Of course."

"She's a water freak," Samuel confirmed. And again Peter saw pride on his face.

"Well, of course! Is there anything more important?" She shook her head, disbelieving. "Not just to animals, you know. Humans are *made* of water, we're *mostly* water." She shook her head again and then left to pack up the leftover food.

Peter turned to Samuel. "You?"

Samuel stared over the river. For a few moments, the only sound was its dancing splash, and Peter thought maybe he shouldn't have asked his question.

But then Samuel answered. "When the war ended, I was lost. See, before I joined the army, I'd been drifting. I'd dumped my family, burned all my friends. I kind of stumbled into the military. Turned out I really liked it. Being part of a group, training together, we made something more than the sum of our parts. What I was doing was important, and other people relied on my doing it right."

After only two full days working as a Warrior, Peter understood. "You didn't want that to end."

"Well, I'm not saying I wanted the war to go on. It was terrible, I saw terrible things. My older brother was killed — he was the only one I was close to in my family." Samuel paused. He raised his hand and rubbed the tattoo on his neck. "People I trained with died. So, no. I didn't miss being at war. But I missed the other parts of it. Community — you know? Purpose. So when I met Jade and she told me about the Water Warriors, I knew it was an answer for me."

Peter realized that he'd never heard Samuel say so much. Samuel looked away, his cheeks flushed, as if he'd just realized the same thing. He got up and rubbed his thighs.

"You turning in?" Peter asked.

Samuel nodded and began to walk away.

Peter picked up the lantern and walked with him toward the pile of sleeping bags. Then something struck him. "Wait. You met Jade *after* all that?"

Samuel stopped and looked over at her. "Last winter."

"*After* your brother and your friends died? You lost those people, you knew what could happen, and you still . . . Why?"

Samuel's eyes widened and he looked like a boy again. "But that *is* why. Without, without . . ." Samuel's hands opened and closed, as if he were trying to grasp words from the air. "If I hadn't loved Jade? Oh, man . . ." He grabbed a fistful of T-shirt and twisted it as if to wrench the idea out of his chest. "I can't even . . . no."

Peter nodded, because he was obviously expected to agree. But inside, all he was thinking was how wrong Samuel had gotten it.

He watched Samuel cross back to where Jade was packing up the cookware and wrap her in a one-armed hug. Jade tipped her head backward into his chin, and she laughed happily at his ambush. But even in the falling dusk, Peter could see that Samuel wasn't laughing. And his fist never left his chest.

17

The kit awoke at midday. She nuzzled sleepily into Pax's chest, and he knew she was seeking her mother's care. He licked her all over gently, as he had seen Bristle do.

After her fur was clean of the dust and grit from their scramble down the cliff, he began on her paws. The little pads were all torn up. She allowed him to pick out shale and flint shards without a whimper, but she flinched each time, and Pax was distressed that he was causing her pain.

When he finished, fresh blood seeped from all four paws. She pulled them in to lick them herself, and Pax could see that her tongue was dry. For that, at least, he could provide relief.

I will carry you to a pond to drink. He eased his jaw around his daughter's neck, but she squirmed free and limped a few steps away from him.

Pax followed. *No. You would leave a blood trail. Predators seek the young, and especially the injured.* He picked her up and this time she did not struggle. He darted across the dried brush to the pond with his daughter jouncing against his chest. He walked into the shallows, surprised again to notice that no quick minnows glittered, no frogs scissored off, and set her down. *The water will soothe your paws.*

Obedient now, the kit stood knee-deep in the water as she drank and drank.

When her belly was taut, Pax carried her to the only greenery he saw, a bed of half-dead juniper. It would make a good temporary refuge — here there were no predators, water to drink only a few steps away.

And then he saw another benefit to the place. *Here, you will learn to swim.*

18

The day was hot — more like July than mid-May — and the terrain was marshy. Peter had drawn sediment duty, and he was slogging along the bank, muddy pant legs chafing his shins, when Jade came up beside him, reached up to unpin her hair, and handed him two clips. "Roll up your cuffs, clip them."

"Oh, thanks. But . . . ?" Peter nodded toward the fallen tangle of her hair, already sticking to her neck.

She shrugged and snapped off a stem from the shadbush beside her. She broke it in two, twisted her hair up into a mound, and speared it through with the twigs. Then she sauntered away to a stand of willows and disappeared into them, waving away mosquitoes.

Peter picked up a fresh sample kit and climbed down the bank to where Samuel was jarring water.

Samuel straightened up and made a stabbing motion to his heart. "Right?"

"What?" Peter asked.

"Kindness. Her hair clips." He raised a glance back to Jade, kneeling in the reeds. "It's like her secret weapon. I still get ambushed."

"Secret weapon?"

"I mean . . . you don't see it coming. Surprise attack. Or maybe that's just me. Maybe the way I grew up, I never expect it. But you'll be hurting about something, or needing something, and she'll say or do this kind thing, and it just *slays* you."

Peter nodded and unzipped the kit. "Secret weapon. I get it."

"Except it heals instead of hurts." Samuel stabbed a thumb at his heart again, smiling this time, and then bent to his work.

Later, when Jade and Samuel were sterilizing the day's equipment at the camp

table, Peter sat at the bank with his bare feet in the cool water. Holding Jade's clips, he thought again about Samuel's comment, that her kindness was like a secret weapon.

Samuel had only meant the stealth of it, not the weapon part. But the strange thing was, lately, whenever anyone had done something kind for him — Vola offering him a home or suggesting his grandfather might move in — he had felt wounded. Or at least felt *at risk* that a wound might be coming.

Which wasn't fair. He knew that. Vola hadn't been trying to hurt him. Jade certainly hadn't when she'd given him those clips — she'd just been her generous self. It suddenly occurred to him that he hadn't even thanked her.

Ashamed, Peter put his boots on again and walked back upstream to where he'd seen a camphor tree. With his jackknife, he hacked off a pencil-thick stem. He cut two six-inch lengths, stripped the bark from them, and then whittled the wood smooth, taking care to round the ends.

He found Jade on the bank near where Samuel was knee-deep in the river. Both of them were frowning down at a rock.

Jade waved and Peter walked over to join her. "Thank you for the clips today." He held out his gift. "Here. For your hair."

"They're beautiful. Thank you." Jade pulled the twigs out of her bun and then refastened it with the polished sticks, smiling.

Peter felt forgiven. "They're camphor wood," he added. "It's what mothballs are made of. So they'll keep the mosquitoes away, too."

Suddenly, Jade pointed at something in the water and Samuel lunged.

"What are you doing?"

"Couple of bog turtles here," Samuel grunted. "Too fast for me."

"They're endangered," Jade explained. "We thought if we could catch one we could draw a blood specimen, see how they're faring. But they're skittish. We can't get near."

"Well, I know how to catch one," Peter offered. "Be right back."

A few yards into the scrub, he located a young black cherry and sawed off a slim branch with his jackknife. He snapped off the side shoots until he had a bare Y on a six-foot length. He bent the two arms of the Y until they met and then wove them back around into a ring about a foot across. Then he stripped off a bunch of slender new shoots from the base of the tree. These he wove across the ring until he had a rough net.

He brought it over.

Jade broke into a grin and waded out with the net. A minute later, when Samuel pointed, she dipped the net and scooped up a turtle. She flipped it belly-up and talked to it in a soothing voice while Samuel pulled out a hypodermic needle and drew a vial of blood.

Then Jade set the turtle back into the river, feet pinwheeling, with a little farewell pat to its shell. She straightened up and bowed her head at Peter.

Peter had to hide a little smile of pride. "It was nothing. In the spring, wild cherry branches are really pliable."

Samuel went up to the camp table to file the specimen. Jade sat on the bank and patted a space beside her for Peter to sit. "You know a lot about trees," she observed.

Peter leaned back on his elbows. "Trees are amazing. You know they communicate with each other?"

"Really? Like humans?"

"Better, actually."

"Better? How?"

Peter almost said, *They don't have to touch*. But he knew how that would sound. "It's better because they don't have to do it directly, tree to tree. That's slow and inefficient. With trees, it's more like a chemical telepathy."

Samuel came down and sat on Peter's other side. "Chemical telepathy?" He raised an eyebrow.

"Really. Like . . . in the savanna, when giraffes start eating an acacia tree, that tree sends out a message underground, through fungus threads — sometimes fungi are a mile long — and all the acacia trees in the neighborhood shoot out a bitter chemical into their leaves so the giraffe leaves them alone. Or, if a tree is in distress, it sends out the message 'Hey, I need help here,' and the other trees send over some sugar or whatever it needs."

"That's amazing." Jade tipped her head back, gazing at the leafy canopy. "A whole community above us, talking to each other underneath us, in a language we can't hear."

"I think humans would evolve to do it if we could. If I were a tree, I could just think, 'Hey, I need help,' and anyone in the area would get the message and send whatever I needed."

Samuel pointed to the net at Peter's feet. "How'd you know how to make that? And do that thing with the birches, and know about camphor repelling bugs?"

"Oh, those things I learned from my . . ." Peter never knew how to refer to Vola. Guardian? Friend? Not family, but pretty close to it. Too close. "This person I've been staying with."

Jade cocked her head. "You don't live with your family?"

Peter suddenly felt trapped, Samuel on one side of him, Jade on the other. Here, in the space between this couple who loved each other, he didn't feel safe. He got up. He made a show of resting the net against a tree, before he answered. "Well . . . my parents are both gone. And my grandfather . . . he's not able."

Jade got to her feet. "What do you mean, your parents are gone?" she asked. Her voice was low and soft the way it had been when she was soothing the turtle. "Oh, no, Peter. Not dead?"

Samuel got up then, too.

Peter stuffed his hands into his pockets. "My mom, when I was seven; my dad, in October." He turned his gaze to the forest across the river, because he knew the expression that would be on both of their faces — every person he'd told at his new school had worn it, every time — and he hated that expression: a mixture of horror and sorrow that made him remember that what had happened *was* awful and sad, and he didn't need to be reminded of that. His hand clenched hard around the jackknife in his pocket.

"This *past* October, Peter?" Jade asked even more quietly. "Just a few months ago?"

He nodded, but still didn't look at her. "He was in the war. People die in wars." He pulled his jackknife from his pocket, rolled it across his palm. "I could cut some twine, make a real net. I bet there are fish . . . fish for dinner . . ."

"You're shaking," Samuel said.

Peter looked down at the jackknife. It was trembling. Or no, it was his hand trembling. His arm. Actually, his whole body, his legs, everything seemed to be vibrating, as if a new, dangerous current were passing through him.

Jade took a step closer. "I think you're saying, 'Hey, I need help here.'"

Peter looked up sharply to see if she was messing with him.

Jade gave him an encouraging smile. She wasn't messing with him. And then she opened her arms, just as if that was a reasonable thing to do.

Time stopped. The last person who had hugged Peter had been his father, a year ago, that last day at the mill right after Peter had let Pax go and he'd gone back down the hill to say goodbye.

A week later, when he'd made it back to Vola's and asked if he could live with her and had to say the words "It will be without my fox," she had tried. He'd knocked her arms away.

His grandfather — well, his grandfather never attempted, not even when they'd gotten the news that Peter's dad had died. It seemed as if the old man's shoulders were rusted and his arms couldn't rise into an embrace.

Peter realized he wasn't breathing. His throat seemed to have swollen shut. He dragged in air, nostrils flared wide, and the air helped but it didn't stop the shaking.

"I'll get that twine," he said, and even his voice was shaking. He stuffed his jackknife back in his pocket and started for the gear box. He really meant to go there, but halfway there, his legs disobeyed.

Peter turned back. He crossed the distance between him and the couple who loved each other. He felt their arms wrap him into the space between them. And that was all right, because probably it made them feel better and besides, he would leave them after the project at the mill to go live alone, and really, how much damage could be done in a few weeks?

For another moment he shook inside that space where they held him. And then he didn't shake.

19

For three days, Pax and the kit rested at the still pond. Each day, Pax left at twilight to hunt on the other side of the ridge where there was game, snatching his prey on the run because his skin prickled with anxiety whenever he could not watch over his kit.

The kit was restless on the first day. She grew irritable when her father would not allow her to explore, when he insisted on carrying her the short distance to the water. After she drank, he waded into the still pond and she followed. When cold water circled her neck, she looked up at him, unsure.

Pax swam away and then turned back and barked for her.

The kit plunged. Once, twice, three times, she thrashed and went under and came up sputtering. But Pax swam by her side, encouraging her with his calm, and soon she was paddling through the water.

On the second day, though, she lay quietly and did not try to leave the nest. He brought her to the pond, and after she'd drunk, Pax urged her to try moving through the water again. She swam listlessly for a while, and then she wanted to be carried back to the nest.

On the third day, she barely lifted her head off the prickly boughs.

That day, Pax found no game, even across the ridge. He hurried back and nudged his daughter awake. *It is time to move on.*

She rose and blinked in the clear rays of the afternoon sun, but then crumpled onto her side, her left hind leg twitching.

Puzzled, Pax checked her over thoroughly. Her paws had healed. He could find no other injuries. He urged her up. *It is not safe here any longer. We will swim across the pond to leave no trail.*

She got up again and staggered after her father to the shore. It did not take long to cross the small pond, but when she reached the shore, the little fox collapsed where she landed and closed her eyes.

Pax shook his fur dry and climbed onto a broad rock to read the wind.

Drifting from the east, it brought news from the river just a short run away: fair weather, no grass fires but a campfire.

And a shock.

His boy. His boy was near.

Peter, gone from him over a year. Peter, whom he had loved for most of his life and then learned to live without, was near.

Pax stilled himself, concentrated, and confirmed: yes, his boy was at the river with another human, maybe two.

His thigh muscles tightened with the old urge to run to him, as though no time had passed, but he held back.

Because time had passed. There had been a long stretch of it — all through the last summer — when Pax had expected Peter to return to find him and bring him home. But that had faded with the summer warmth, and by fall, he'd come to understand that his home was with Bristle, wherever it was that she felt safe. And when he'd settled in the Deserted Farm with her, he'd stopped watching for Peter completely.

The breeze freshened. A new sweet scent, mingled with the smell of wood fire and of his boy, triggered a memory.

When he'd been very young, Pax had gone with Peter and his father to live in the woods for a few days in a small cloth house by a stream. His boy's father had built a fire, and they'd cooked food, and Peter had shared his food with Pax. Later the humans had held sticks over the coals, and a warm, sweet smell — strange but appealing — had arisen from their white tips and Pax had watched Peter and his father eat the good-smelling white tips.

Tempted, Pax had darted in and snatched up a stick Peter had laid on a stone beside him. He had yelped, surprised by how hot the marshmallow was, smeared over his snout. And his boy had leaped up, stripped off his shirt and soaked it in the stream, then held the cool cloth over Pax's muzzle, soothing him and hugging him. Pax had felt safe and loved.

Pax drew in the wind again. He found the scent of the boy he missed. And he decided.

He bounded over to his daughter and nudged her awake. *We are leaving now. It is not far to the river.*

She rose, but he could see that she was still exhausted from the swim across the pond. He would have to carry her, and to travel encumbered that way he would need the benefit of light.

He led her to a clump of dried bluestem grass. *Rest now. We will leave at dawn.*

20

"This is the last of them." Samuel held out the bag of marshmallows along with three willow sticks. Peter took a stick and threaded a marshmallow. The night was chilly, the fire had died to embers, it was a perfect time for them.

Watching it brown, he was struck by a memory. For his eighth birthday, his dad had taken him camping, and had allowed him to bring Pax. The weekend had been great, but the last night, sitting around a fire, Peter had made a mistake: he'd laid a marshmallow down to cool beside him, and Pax had snatched it up. Peter had wrapped the young fox's burnt snout in a wet T-shirt quickly, but afterward he'd felt so terrible that he told his father he thought he didn't deserve to have a pet.

"Well, that's not how I see it," his father had answered. He'd pointed at Pax, sleeping on Peter's lap. "And I don't think that's how your fox sees it, either. See, I think it's just the opposite. An accident happened, and you jumped up and took good care of your pet. You were responsible. That's how I see it. Maybe your fox just knew that when he was hurt, you made it better."

At eight, it had seemed a shocking insight — that a single act could be viewed different ways — and Peter had fallen asleep pondering it. Actually, even at nearly fourteen, it still seemed kind of a magic trick.

Beside him, Samuel stood up and broke Peter's reverie. He handed out the three pairs of boots that had been drying by the fire. "We should get some sleep," he said. "We have to leave before dawn tomorrow."

Peter tugged on his boots. "How come?"

"The first crew of Water Warriors will be setting out from the reservoir tomorrow. We've got a lot of ground to cover in the next few days to make it to the next site before they get there. We should turn in early."

"I'll be glad to go," Jade said, although she didn't make a move to get up. "This is the place, Peter. That pond I told you about is just west of here. I don't like remembering about those raccoons."

She checked her boots, then placed them back by the coals. "Still wet." She shivered, and Peter thought maybe she was imagining what might have happened to the raccoon babies, but that wasn't it. She leaned over her feet and squeezed her toes. "They're always cold," she lamented. "And look at these army-issue socks. Give me some real wool!"

Samuel laughed in agreement. "True. Always cold."

But Peter grew still. He pulled his marshmallow from the fire and set it aside.

Another memory stabbed him: when he was little, his mother used to read to him in his bed, Peter curled on his side to see the illustrations. Halfway through the story, she would inch her bare feet under his knees, saying, "Icicles! Brrr . . ." And it was true, her feet were cold. But Peter always held his knees over them, and she always made a big deal of marveling at how warm they were, and he always glowed with little-boy pride.

For a minute, he imagined offering his knees to Jade. He would do it with a no-big-deal shrug, because it would just be an act of kindness, and who would understand kindness more than this girl? It would be okay.

But no, maybe it wouldn't be okay. The sensation of another's body touching his, even through clothing. Sometimes Vola would brush his shoulder or rest her hand over his when she was showing him how to use a tool, and even those things shook him a little. Yesterday's hug felt like it had broken something inside him, and he couldn't tell whether that was a good thing or not.

Just then, Jade stretched a leg out, tapped her toes on his hip. "Icicles, brrr . . ." She laughed.

Peter felt his throat tighten. He locked his chin, squeezed his lids against the tears, turned his face away. "I'm tired," he said. "I'll unpack the bedrolls."

He rose, but Jade jumped to her feet and stayed him with a hand to his wrist. "I'm sorry. Whatever it was I said."

Peter scrubbed a palm across his eyes. "It's the smoke. You didn't say anything wrong. And I'm tired is all. A lot of hiking today."

"Sure. I'm still sorry. It's just that . . . You're a very serious boy. I guess I wanted to see you laugh. Go get some sleep."

Peter made his escape. He washed up and then spread out a bedroll, choosing a spot on the far side of the fire on a hard, flat stretch of rock covered in lichen.

He removed the box holding his father's ashes from his pack. He set it carefully at the pillow end and tucked his sweatshirt around it. Then he crawled in, turned his back to the fire, and zipped up the bedroll all the way.

21

Although the distance from the still pond was not far, it was already full light when Pax and his daughter reached the river. She had wanted to walk herself, but whenever she tried, she soon fell over on her side, looking bewildered. She struggled whenever Pax tried to pick her up, but even when she finally relented and allowed him to carry her, she whimpered if he ran or even trotted, so they had to travel slowly.

Now, he let her down gently onto a welter of smooth roots beside the riverbank. He watched as she took in their new surroundings.

The air smelled of moss and ferns and cold campfire — Peter and the other humans were at least an hour gone. Chickadees bickered over the last winter pinecones high above them, bark beetles scuttled in the dead elm beside them, and water splashed quietly over a stony patch of riverbed below.

River, he explained. *Flowing water is powerful. We must stay at the shallow edge.*

Expecting his curious daughter to take off down the bank to explore, he readied himself to follow.

The kit only dropped her head to her paws and closed her eyes. Her breaths grew slower. But suddenly her eyes flew open and she scrambled to her feet again.

You are scenting humans, Pax confirmed. *They are gone.* Again he invited her to explore. *River?*

The kit refused the offer. She dropped down again, curled herself up tight between the roots, and fell asleep.

After testing the air to be certain there were no predators nearby, Pax left her to discover what he could about his boy, here only hours ago.

Peter, Pax learned, was healthy. He was traveling with two other humans, a female and another male, and there had been no aggression between them. Their paths followed the river: they had entered from the north and left for the south. While he had stopped here, his boy had eaten beside a wood fire — Pax could smell traces of meat and of marshmallows. He tracked down three stripped branches bearing remnants of the sticky prize on their tips, covered with ants.

Next, Pax examined the clearing where Peter had slept. His boy had chosen the spot well — there was a good view of the river and the lichen bed was dry and free of all but the most harmless insects. Pax dipped his snout and breathed in the scent of the boy he had loved.

He flicked a glance over to his sleeping daughter and felt again the urge to teach her the important things he had learned. He trotted back and nudged her awake. *Follow me.*

The kit rose obediently, but her gait was even more unsteady. He picked her up, and she allowed this without complaint.

As soon as he placed her on the bed of lichen, though, she leaped away. Her ears were flattened in alarm and the fur on her neck stood up.

Pax called for her to come back.

She refused.

He carried her to the spot again.

Humanden! she protested, backing farther away. *Humans. Dangerous.*

Yes. Most.

The kit didn't come any closer, but she sat down. *Most?*

Pax knew that his daughter was stubborn, like her mother, so he waited while she took this in. At last he saw her relax her guard.

He nosed the scent on the lichen. *Not this one. My boy.*

Her sharp ears cocked in question.

Pax lay down. *Come here.*

After a moment, the kit crept to him cautiously and settled down against the white fur of his chest.

Pax dropped his paw over her shoulder. *When I was a new kit, newer than you, I was very ill. It was a time before remembering. It was knowing. A human boy took me out of my den.*

The kit's eyes widened. *Mother-father allowed?*

Mother-father were gone. This boy brought me to his den. He fed me and warmed me close to his skin.

This boy was mother-father?

Pax considered this. *Yes,* he agreed. *Mother-father. Later, Friend. This human used only a soft voice with me. His hands held me safe, but never grasped tight. When I called for him, he came. I could trust him.*

The kit was quiet. Pax knew she was weighing this information against her mother's warnings.

She dropped her muzzle and drew in Peter's scent. *How can you know humans' intent?*

Human intent is expressed in their faces, their scents, their voices, their gestures.

Like foxes?

Yes, like foxes. But they can be false-acting.

How do you know which humans can be trusted?

Pax thought. *Watch them carefully, for a long time. They will show you.*

22

Samuel had drawn the short straw and had trudged off through the underbrush to find the feeder springs. Peter and Jade were collecting water and sediment at the main current — a calm, mossy stretch, glinting green.

Jade climbed out and handed Peter a jar. She leaned against a trunk beside the camp table and looked over the water. "This must be the most perfect hundred yards of river ever."

Labeling the jar, Peter smiled. "Samuel says you say the same thing at every bend. He says, 'That girl sure loves running water.'"

Jade nodded. "I do love rivers. But I really love this one. Oh, I know it isn't much in size, as rivers go. Only a dozen feet wide in some places. Enough not to be downgraded to a stream, but not by much, right? What it lacks in size, though, it makes up for in determination."

"Determination? What do you mean?"

"It's always moving. Never lets anything stop it up. As if it knows blocked water goes stagnant."

Peter put down the jar, looking at the river with new interest. He liked listening to Jade.

"And this river is special. See, this one is mine."

"Yours?"

"My grandparents lived on this river, about sixty miles down. Well, they still do — it's a tiny little town that didn't see any battles and everybody had wells, so nobody left. I spent every summer with them when I was a kid. I had a rowboat and I knew every bend, every beaver dam, every swans' nest. That made it mine."

Jade took a fresh jar and splashed back in. For an hour, they settled into an easy rhythm. The river murmured quietly in the late afternoon sunshine. It sounded patient, in no hurry. Peter felt he was drifting with its peaceful current.

Until Jade startled him with a tap on his elbow. Peter looked down at the sample case in his hand. "Did I pack this one wrong?"

Jade shook her head and rolled her eyes to a pine bough above them. "See that guy?" she whispered. "The chickadee? I think he's getting ready to pay us a visit."

Peter located the bird, at least a dozen feet up, studying them intently. "Well, he's not afraid, because he's got wings," he confirmed. "But I don't think he'll get any closer."

"No, really. He's been hanging around since we unpacked. He's curious. If we give him half a chance, he'll come right over. Watch." Jade eased a granola bar out of her pocket, held it up as if to show the bird, then peeled down the wrapper with small moves.

She lowered herself cross-legged to the ground and patted a space next to her. Peter put down his marker and eased himself into a comfortable position beside her to watch.

Jade surprised him. "You do it," she whispered. She broke off a few bits of granola bar and placed them in Peter's hand, then pocketed the rest. She lifted his arm, palm up. "See? Friends," she called to the bird. "We can keep talking," she said to Peter, "but soft and easy, okay? And no sudden moves."

They sat like that for a moment, three creatures watching each other. Then Jade turned her head slightly to Peter. "Sometimes, don't you get the feeling they're trying to make a connection with us? As if they're saying, 'Hey, you get hungry, I get hungry, we have so much in common!'"

Peter nodded. "When I had my fox . . ." He looked out over the river, giving himself a moment for the lump to swell up in his throat and choke off the words. The lump didn't gather. "When I had my fox, people used to tell me the same story all the time. 'I was walking in the woods and I noticed a fox off to the side. As if it just happened to be walking the same direction, that's all.' The people always described the way the fox was looking at them as . . . well, companionable, you know? Equals. Then the person kept walking and forgot about it, until a while later, the person looked over and . . . there was the fox again. And again. Everyone said the same thing: it was as if the fox was saying, 'Hey, I'm on a walk, you're on a walk, we're walking together, cool.'"

The bird hopped down a few branches, craning its head out to better inspect the offering in Peter's hand.

"I've had that happen, too," Jade said. "Squirrels, crows. Once, a fawn followed me until its mother put an end to that, which, you can't blame her, since we eat them."

Peter watched the chickadee drift down to the lowest limb. It gave a peck to its shoulder feathers, then cocked its head to study him with a quick black eye.

Peter lowered his voice even more. "They all said they felt *chosen* by that, as if the fox had made a decision that they were worth trusting."

The chickadee side-walked to the very end of the bough, swaying on a slim spray of pine needles. Peter and Jade stopped talking. They looked at each other, as if to give their visitor privacy.

Out of the corner of his eye, Peter saw the bird make its move. He felt it land on the tip of his longest finger, felt the tiny claws tighten to perch.

Jade froze, except to hike her eyebrows at Peter in delight. Peter hiked his back at her, and felt a silent laugh warm his whole body. Jade slowly turned her face to beam a smile at the bird as it ate. That smile, Peter thought, would cut across any species line.

The chickadee ruffled its chest feathers and flew off, and Peter laughed out loud. It struck him: this was Jade's kindness again. Her secret weapon. She'd given him a moment with a wild creature, and now he was a boy who laughed.

Jade pulled out the rest of the granola bar, broke it in half, and held out a piece to Peter. "Communion. With a bird. Can you believe how lucky we are?"

Peter took a bite and ate it thoughtfully. "Vola called me lucky when she heard that I'd raised a fox. She said not many people get to have that kind of a bond with a wild animal. She called it a 'two but not two' bond. Connected. It's a Buddhist idea."

Jade nodded. "Nondualism. I know that concept. So, will you get another pet when you go back?"

"Go back?"

"Home. To this Vola's. When your service is finished."

Maybe it was the chickadee, maybe it was the river murmuring sleepily — something lulled Peter into letting down his guard. "I'm not going back," he said. "My old home is just past that mill. I'm going there."

Jade sat back. "But . . . who's there?"

"Nobody now. But when the Water Warriors are finished, people will come back."

"No. I mean . . ." Jade folded her hands on her lap, as if she was trying to calm something. "You're thirteen. You can't live alone."

Peter grew wary. "Oh, I meant . . . no, sure. I meant I'm not going back *right away*. First I . . . I'm going to spread my dad's ashes. And see about the house, you know. That's all. I'll be there a couple of weeks, I meant."

Jade eyed him for a moment longer than he liked, but she let it go. "Well, maybe

152

that's the place you'll get a pet. As soon as you open up the house, you won't be alone, that's for sure."

"What do you mean?"

"Where people had to relocate, animals were abandoned. They'll come around when they sense you're back."

Except not at his house, Peter knew. Pax had marked his yard for five years — no cats or dogs ever ventured in. "No. That won't happen. I don't want another pet."

Jade looked at him sharply again. She opened her mouth, but just then Samuel returned.

"Storm tomorrow," he said. "We should head out early."

Peter jumped up and helped him off with his gear. For the next hour, he kept busy recording data, gathering wood, building the fire. He helped pack up the equipment, then volunteered for cook duty. He set a tin of beans on the fire and pretended to be engrossed in stirring them. At last, he passed out plates and they ate, then cleaned up.

All through it, Peter felt Jade watching him.

The two foxes watched the world come awake from a mossy hollow. Red-winged blackbirds claimed territory in the willow scrub across the river, chipmunks scurried for overlooked acorns in the leaf litter around the dead oak, shad flies lifted off the water like curls of fog. Finally came the visitors Pax most needed.

A pair of crows dropped into the bare oak, followed quickly by another and another until the tree was alive with their conversation.

Listen, Pax instructed his kit. *Crows travel quickly and far. They know everything that is happening. And they are generous — they share the news.*

154

Crouching low with their tails down to assure the crows that they meant no threat, Pax and the kit walked to the base of the tree and settled.

What do you hear?

The kit concentrated. *They are upset.*

Yes. Why?

Humans. A large flock coming down the river from the north.

Pax and his kit listened intently, and were rewarded with much information. These humans, they learned, were the ones who had camped at the reservoir. Among them were a few youths. They were moving slowly, the crows reported. They seemed peaceful, but they were carrying equipment like the war-sick humans of last year.

Pax got up and began to pace. Slow-moving humans could become fast-moving at any time. Peaceful humans could become aggressive without notice.

He felt trapped. He had smelled a new human-set fire the day before, off to the east this time, so traveling along the river was still safest. More importantly, the water would hide their tracks from coyotes or bears. That meant he had only two choices: follow the river north, back to Bristle and home, or south to the Broad Valley, then circle home from there. Heading north he would encounter the large group of humans; south, he might meet Peter and his two companions.

Although the pull to return to his family was strong, there was not really a choice. The large group of humans presented a possible danger. Peter would never harm them, and would not allow his two companions to try.

Pax returned to his kit, who was now listening to the crows chattering about a barn whose roof had been torn off in a storm, exposing a mountain of corn. *We are leaving.*

Home?

Not yet. First we will go to the Broad Valley.

Pax felt an urge to hurry, but his daughter needed nourishment for the trip ahead. He led her along the bank, where he had found the rank odor of snapping turtle.

Pax showed her a likely spot of soft dirt and dug. A few inches down, he began scooping out leathery eggs in uncountable numbers. Pax filled his belly quickly and encouraged his daughter to eat as much as she could.

The kit rolled an egg around, then laid her head on her paws.

Pax popped a leathery shell under her nose, spilling the yolk.

She lapped at it tentatively, and then gulped it. She reached for another and broke it herself, lapping happily. She ate another and another and another, and Pax was relieved. It had been a few days since she had eaten, and now her belly was round.

It was time.

Pax assessed the muddy riverbank and then the higher dry ground. He did not like wet paws, but traveling in the water would provide the most protection from dangers. And so they set out down the river — sometimes in reeds, sometimes in pebbly shallows, and sometimes deeper, where the current made swimming almost effortless. Always silent as fish.

24

The storm had hit with a sudden volley of hail, hard as gunshot, then settled into a gusty downpour. Peter had shown Jade and Samuel how to make a lean-to of thick cedar boughs, and they'd crouched under it most of the day, sodden but grateful they weren't out in the open getting lashed.

When it finally ended, they changed into dry clothes and built a fire with the bundle of reeds Peter had thought to cut in the morning and had carried with him, wedged down the back of his rain gear.

The reeds caught in hot flares, but the wood smoked and hissed. The sulky fire cheered them, though, and after eating cold biscuits and jerky, all three were sitting side by side on a single log in front of it.

Jade pulled out a book, and Peter and Samuel started whittling to pass the time. After a minute, Peter realized Samuel had put down his knife and was just watching him. "That's quite a knife. And you're really good with it."

"No, it's all the knife," Peter demurred. "It's really old, but it's the best." And it was. It had been Vola's, but she'd given it to him and he'd barely been without it since. Besides being beautiful, with carved nickel bolsters and a maple handle, it was a fine knife — steady in the palm, clever in the wood.

"Here," he said, holding it out to Samuel. "Try it."

Samuel took the knife with the grin of a kid on Christmas morning, and Peter leaned back. He was thinking how easily they had become a team in just a week, when they heard a tone from the radio kit.

Samuel dropped the knife and jumped up. "That's the emergency alert." He pulled the radio out of his pack, carried it into a clearing, and bent over the crackle.

159

After a while, Samuel packed the radio up and came back to the fire. "The mill operation is pushed off a week at least, maybe two. The storm surge compromised a dam upriver and our platoon is being diverted there."

"Are we supposed to join them?" Jade asked.

"No, they've left. They couldn't wait."

Jade and Samuel looked at each other, and Peter saw something secret pass between them.

"Does that mean . . . ?" Jade asked, a smile beginning to curl.

"Yep," Samuel agreed. "We're free until they get here, so . . ."

Jade clapped both hands over her mouth, an expression of unexpected joy.

Samuel lifted his shoulders in a *why not?* gesture, and he looked pretty happy, too.

"What?" Peter asked.

"We were going to beg for a few days' leave after the mill assignment," Jade said. "We want to go to my grandparents' place and get married. See, my gramma's not that healthy, so we don't want to wait. And now, well . . . we can do it right away." She looked up at Samuel. "Are we still supposed to get the gear to the mill?"

Samuel shook his head. "Another silver lining. Don't have to navigate those rapids tomorrow."

As usual, Jade expanded on Samuel's few words. "The last stretch, just before the old mill site. The river drops fifty feet over a spread of just a hundred yards. It was going to be really dangerous."

"I know that place," Peter said. "We used to play around in those rapids when I was a kid. It's not so bad."

"It's different now," Jade said. "Last fall, they blew up a bridge just above the old mill, destabilized the whole area. Also, that was a lot of rain." She gestured to the river. "It's already swollen a foot higher than it should be."

She turned to Samuel. "So what do we do with the gear?"

"They want us to lock everything at a guard station at the Route Seven intersection tomorrow morning."

Jade brightened. "That's on the way. We can spend a whole week with my grandparents, do it right." She plucked at her grubby cargo pants. "Civilization! Hit a thrift shop, find myself a real dress!"

She tapped Peter's thigh. "You'll come with us, of course. My grandparents have a big old house, plenty of room, and you'll be our guest of honor."

Peter leaned away. He carefully wrapped up the last biscuits, weighing the idea. But he knew the answer. "I can't," he said, handing Jade the food. "I guess we should pack up."

Jade's disappointment looked real. "Okay, then. Sure. Samuel, radio back, see if they can pick Peter up when they get the stuff. Return him to his platoon."

"No, don't," Peter said. "I'll go to my old house and get started moving in. There's a lot to do —"

Jade narrowed her eyes.

And too late, he realized what he'd said.

"Samuel," Jade said without taking her gaze from Peter, "would you take care of the pack-up? I'd like a few minutes alone with our friend."

Jade stared at him, eyebrows raised, as Samuel left. In the silence, Peter could hear the dull thunder of the rapids, far off but ominous. He shifted away, eyeing the sleeping bags. He could say he was tired, had a headache —

"Moving in?" Jade put her hand over his, as if she knew he was ready to bolt. "I get it now," she said quietly. "I see what you're doing."

Her hand felt steady and soft and not dangerous. Which felt dangerous to him. But he didn't bolt.

"No pets. Not going back to that Vola. Going to start living on your own in a deserted town. Nobody to care about, nobody caring about you, right? No one else will get in," she said. Little flames from the fire were reflected in her eyes.

Peter didn't answer. Of course he thought that. That was exactly what he wanted to happen.

"But it doesn't work that way. That won't make you safe. It will kill you."

Peter's head snapped up.

"No, you won't stop breathing, or anything like that. But you'll stop living, in ways that are important, anyway."

Peter slid a thumbnail under the bark of the log and pried off a strip, considering.

Actually, it would be okay if he stopped living in those ways Jade thought were important. Out here in the woods, he'd seen that a big part of living was just surviving, getting your jobs done. Living by himself, that part could be enough. That part could be plenty. Out here, everything he did seemed simple and clear. Out here, he worked so hard he was too tired to think about the things that hurt inside when he crawled into his bed. He could live like this just fine.

"Besides," Jade said, "good luck with that. Someone will get in. A little sliver of caring. The tiniest crack in your shell is all it takes. You won't even see it coming."

Peter thought about Vola, how close he'd come to letting her be like a family. How quickly he'd let his guard down with this couple.

But he was watching now. He would be watching all the time now. He would see it coming.

Jade got up. She stretched, opening her arms wide as if to embrace the whole forest. "Big day tomorrow. And a big week — I'm getting married! I'd better get some sleep."

After she left, Peter stayed where he was. He sat on the log a long time, long enough for the fire to die to embers and the cold to seep through his jeans and numb the back of his thighs. He watched the stars emerge, and as his eyes adjusted to the dark, he saw bats swooping silently over the river's surface, feeding. At his feet, a swarm of ants was already working the biscuit crumbs.

He felt hopeful suddenly, as if these small creatures doing their normal things were showing him how simple his life could be. As if it was a sign.

He watched the ants form a line carrying their tiny prizes, followed their progress to a crack in the bark at the far end of the log.

Inside then, right underneath him, was the colony. There would be chambers for eggs, storage vaults for food, a room for the queen — a whole community expanding inside this dead log. A little crack was all it took. This log hadn't seen it coming.

Peter got up. Turned out, he didn't believe in signs.

25

Pax had smelled the storm coming. *That is the scent of rain, distant,* he'd taught his kit. *That is wind gathering itself before lashing free.*

Danger? she wanted to know as the first thunder cracked the air.

No. Power, but no menace.

When it struck with a surprising volley of cold hail, he'd led her to cover in a dense thicket, but as soon as it lessened to rain, they'd moved on. Pax taught his daughter to wear the storm on her fur and flare her nostrils into its vigor.

The next day, the travel went well. The kit became better at moving. She learned to predict the wobble on her left side and compensate for it, and she fell less often. Determined to keep up with her father, she needed less rest, as if she were recovering from whatever illness had befallen her at the still pond.

Along the way, she grew curious again, and Pax showed her many things about the world.

She grew hungry again, too. What she wanted was eggs, only eggs. They gorged themselves from plentiful spring nests — more snapping turtle, also bufflehead and wood duck and goose. Seeing her eat eased Pax's worries.

Every time they stepped onto shore, Pax found that his boy had passed through recently, and was still healthy. This knowledge always brought him comfort as well.

Then Pax heard a sound.

He recognized it: water pounding granite. It had been a softer rumble then, but he knew it came from the place on the river where Gray had died and Runt had lost his leg and Pax had left his boy, not far from the Broad Valley.

Food would be plentiful at that Broad Valley; his kit would continue to strengthen there. They could return for Bristle and the rest of the family soon.

For another hour they walked beside the river, which was flowing faster now, until dawn pinked the eastern sky, and the kit began to tire.

Pax found a protected spot beneath a stone overhang and chose a patch of springy moss for a bed. As he curled up with the kit, he listened again to the sound. Still half an hour's journey away, the rush of falling water was much louder.

The kit sensed his uneasiness.

Dangerous? she wanted to know.

To that, Pax had no answer.

26

Peter stood near the edge, looking down. It looked nothing like the falls of only a year ago: those falls had rattled peacefully over a few big ledges in the middle that were so stable you could leap from them. Now, the vast water poured and crashed, poured and crashed, as though furious.

"We turn in here," Samuel called. "Come on."

Peter was glad to leave. But when the three of them pushed out of the last thicket onto a dirt road, his whole body tensed, as if expecting a punch. "This is the service road to the old mill, isn't it," he said. It wasn't a question. This road would take them right by the place his father had forced him to abandon Pax.

Samuel nodded. "Used to go there. It hasn't been used since the bridge got blown up, but it's still clear on this side. It'll be a breeze after the rough hiking we've had."

Samuel was right — the travel was easy. But it was uncomfortably quiet. All morning, Jade kept stealing looks at Peter, Samuel kept stealing looks at Jade stealing looks at Peter, and Peter kept pretending he didn't notice either.

Until two hours later, he drew up short, a hand to his gut.

It had been a year, and there was nothing to distinguish the spot from the miles of trees and weeds they'd just passed, but he was sure: this was the place he'd driven away from Pax. He knew it. Or maybe this place knew him. Maybe places had memories. He crouched and shook a handful of gravel through his fingers.

"What is it, Peter?" Jade asked, stopping. "Is something wrong?"

For a second, he considered not answering her. But he'd already done enough to be ashamed of here. "I did something bad here, once," he said, looking into the woods.

Samuel turned around at that. He and Jade waited, as if they weren't going anywhere until he explained himself.

And Peter dropped his pack and told them about it. The whole story of abandoning Pax. The wretched drive, knowing he was going to have to betray his pet. The big lie of throwing the toy soldier. And how butchered he'd felt when his father hit the gas, as if he'd left a chunk of his own heart bleeding on that dusty road. Seeing Pax running at top speed after them until he fell back exhausted. "I went back for him, though. I went back and I found him."

He shouldered his pack. "Let's go. I don't want to be here anymore." He started down the road.

Jade caught up with him. "Wait. I'm just putting it together. If this is where you left your fox, and you told me you saw your dad when you went back for him . . . Your dad must have been stationed at the old mill. That's where you last saw your father, is that right?"

Peter nodded, a lump swelling in his throat. "Let's go. Please."

"So it's also where you set your fox free, right?"

Peter nodded again, head down.

"You lost them both at that mill site."

The woods seemed to grow silent; even the birds stopped their songs.

"Peter," Jade asked very quietly, "are you really going to serve at the mill site with the Water Warriors?"

And the truth struck him. He hadn't admitted it, but no, of course he couldn't do that. He could never set foot in that place again.

"Peter? Are you?"

He shook his head miserably without looking up.

"Were you ever going to?"

"I don't know. No, I guess not," he admitted. "But now you know why."

"I'm sorry," Jade said.

Peter was relieved at how easily she understood. "Thanks."

"No," Jade said, both her hands up, *stop*. "I mean, I get it. That's a terrible place for you. You're angry and you're afraid. Really, really afraid. But sorry, I don't think you can go around it. You're grieving. I know something about that. You have to feel your way into it, and then feel your way out. And you're brave enough for that."

"I don't think so."

"I know so. It will be hard. But you won't be alone. We'll be there. And doing something so good will go a long way to change your feelings about the place. From then on it will also be the place where you helped clean the water, make it okay for the people and the animals to come back. It will be that story, too."

"Maybe," Peter said. And then he started walking again, taking the lead so they couldn't see his face.

27

The sound was now a roar. Pax looked out, but all he could see through the reeds was a flat expanse of calm-looking water.

Stay here, he ordered the kit. And then he waded in to get a clearer view.

A hundred yards down water, the river dropped away. He swam out to the middle.

Too late, he felt it — a tug on his legs first, then a deep drag against his chest and hips, pulling him toward the brink. He began paddling back to the bank. At first, he was only surprised not to make any headway. He paddled harder and lost ground, and he became afraid.

He heard a cry. He turned. The kit. She was in the water behind him, struggling to keep her head above the surface, coming up fast. As she swept by, he lunged.

With her shoulder in his mouth, the river dragged harder. He clamped down for a better grip and she yowled. He tried to adjust his bite, but just as he did, she twisted. His daughter was torn from his jaws. Pax snapped at her tumbling form, but caught only water.

She spun away, her eyes rolling white in terror, and then she disappeared below the surface. An instant later, Pax heard her scream from the edge of the water and there he saw a flash of red fur. And then nothing.

Gasping, Pax let the current carry him to the edge. And there, just for an instant, he saw: on either side the land fell away and fell away in great ripped chasms, the river raged and thundered downward. And he was over.

Down he went, into the churning water, until he slammed hard against a ledge. He scrabbled for purchase, found it, lost it, got his legs on another outcropping and held on, claws to rock. From there he searched wildly for his lost child, but could not find her. And then a wall of water hit him broadside, knocking his lungs flat.

The fox swallowed river. And the river swallowed fox.

28

For another couple of hours they hiked in silence, Peter's father's ashes banging on his back a little harder at the quick pace. The only thing he let himself think about was how close to home he was. He'd make it there by tomorrow morning, for sure.

At last, they came to the guardhouse. Jade and Samuel unlocked it and went in to store the gear. Peter stayed outside, remembering how here, last year, a guard had come running out when Peter had come by. The guard had been all business until Peter told him he was going in for his pet, and then he'd started talking about how he was worried about his own dog and brought out a photo. The guard looked completely different gazing down at that worn photo. He looked like what he was — a kid, worrying about his dog. And after that, he'd let Peter go through, wishing him well.

With a start, Peter realized that Jade and Samuel were standing beside him.

Jade was holding what was left of the food. A box of cornbread mix, three hard biscuits, half a bag of dried apples, a small canned ham. "We won't need this," she said. "You will."

Peter took it with a nod. He hadn't thought about food, but now he remembered that his dad had cleaned out the house before they left. "Not leaving any mice bait," he'd said.

Samuel scuffed a boot. "So, I guess it's goodbye."

"Just for a while," Jade added. "See you in a week or so. At the mill."

"Sure." Peter had to turn away to lie. "See you in a week or so."

They shouldered their packs and Peter followed them to the intersection. He watched Jade take Samuel's hand, and just like that, they were a "they" and he was all alone. That was what he wanted, he reminded himself. Still, he felt an actual chill, as if a cold wind had blown down his collar.

"Wait! Happy wedding," he cried as they crossed.

They turned and waved to him. "Hey, remember," Jade called. "You watch out for that sliver."

29

He found her.

He couldn't see her through the spray. He couldn't hear any cries over the water's roar. He couldn't scent her over the wild smells of a freed river loaded with bounty. He found her with a sense deeper than those, too deep to be named. *Daughter. There*, it directed the fox.

There was a tree. A hundred years old, its core rotted through by borers. The storm surge had ripped it out by its roots a mile upriver and left it half-submerged at the bottom of the rapids.

Caught in its tangled roots was a very small fox.

Pax stood in rushing shallows. His child dangled by her shoulders just beyond his reach. He barked up in gladness and fear. For another moment, she hung as empty and lifeless as a pelt. And then she opened her eyes.

Pax barked again, all joy this time. He splashed underneath her, assessing their positions. Just past the shallows, the current crashed over jagged rock. If he missed his landing, they would be swept away.

He would not miss.

He leaped and caught purchase, hung on just long enough to tug his child free. He dropped into the shallows with her locked in his jaws, and pulled her clear of the water.

He nestled her on a hummock of grass and curled himself around her, reassuring her she was safe. And she was. She was sodden and limp, but she was not bleeding, and her limbs seemed unbroken.

What Pax wanted most was to bring her home. The warmth of that den with her brothers and mother would stop her shaking. Bristle would surround their daughter with her fierce protection, would feed her own strength to her kit.

Bristle's presence would soothe Pax, too. He longed for it — since meeting her, he had never spent this much time away from her. But the path home to Bristle was fraught with dangers, and even if none were encountered, the walking alone was too arduous for a kit as battered and exhausted as his.

There was no going home yet. He needed a shelter for her here and now.

And he knew of one.

Not twenty full-bounds away, just up from the river bank. An ancient hemlock whose boughs swept the ground, making a piney grotto underneath, where Pax had once sheltered with the old fox, Gray. Dark but airy, cushioned with many seasons of soft pine duff, whose scent would mask their own from predators.

Before bringing her inside, he dried her with his tongue and left her in a sunny spot to warm. Then he circled the tree, nose to the ground, scenting for dangers. He found none, but noticed something else: for the first time since reaching the river, he did not scent his boy. Peter's tracks had stopped abruptly at the brink of the rapids.

Pax hurried back to his kit and carried her inside the hemlock's skirt. He settled her near the massive trunk and lay down close beside her, alert to her every movement. Even after she fell asleep, he watched her breathing, until at last he dropped his head over hers and closed his eyes.

Only then did he sense his own injuries — a dull ache in his shoulder, his hip, right hind leg, a sharper pain in his side when he breathed deeply.

The kit whimpered in a dream and bucked into his chest. And Pax understood once again that for her, he would do whatever was needed.

30

Peter found the front door key where it had always been left and let himself in. He pulled open the curtains on the living room window beside him and stood blinking for a moment.

Everything was exactly the same, only dulled by a year-thick layer of dust. But at the same time, somehow everything also looked foreign. Or maybe unreal. He tried the kitchen. There, he had the same unsettled feeling — as if someone had gone to a lot of trouble to replicate his old home, but had gotten everything slightly wrong.

Hands on the counter to steady himself, he took a few breaths. It's just stuff, he told himself. Just some cupboards and pots and pans. Some couches and chairs. Just *things*, and yes, his parents had used them back when they were alive and that was what was spooking him. Maybe it wouldn't feel like his home anymore, maybe it didn't suit him as well as the cabin he'd built, but this was his place now.

He walked out of the kitchen. In the back hall, the door to his father's room stood half-open. He yanked it closed without looking inside.

The next room was his. At least he'd feel okay in there. His room had always been a refuge. He pushed open the door, and was immediately hit with the looming presence of all that he'd lost since the last time he'd been inside.

It's just a room, he told himself. And he walked in and faced it down.

Pax's favorite toys in the corner, on the blanket he used to nap on. His collar on the windowsill. Baseball trophies lined up on the bureau with the watch Peter never wore and the cap he barely took off; ball game ticket stubs tucked into the mirror; crumpled notices from school on the floor. The orange juice he'd drunk that final morning last spring, dried now to a brown disk at the bottom of the glass beside his old rocket ship lamp.

Everything from a time when he was a normal kid, a stupid normal kid who had thought that things couldn't get worse after you lost a mother.

He opened his bureau drawers, his closet, and then slammed them shut on all the stupid clothes the stupid kid had worn back then.

Peter dropped to his bed. He wrapped his arms around his chest and he felt they were the only things holding his heart in.

When his mom died, Peter's father had gone around the house gathering up everything of hers to throw away. Peter had scrambled along beside him, not understanding how his father would want to be without them. Now he understood. He got it now, all right.

Maybe he should burn it all. Make a big fire, burn everything that could remind him of his old life.

He left the room and walked out the back door. Here, in the backyard, he could set the blaze. Make a base of kindling — dead branches from winter storms all around, pile it with hay, load all his stuff, then . . .

Peter checked the shed, and yes, a can of lighter fluid was on the top shelf. He pulled it down, and a knife clattered to the floor.

He picked it up. It was nearly identical to the jackknife he'd gotten from Vola — the one in his backpack right now. For a second he wished he could show this one to her, and then he wished he could ask his father where it had come from, how come he'd never seen it, but he pushed those thoughts aside.

He flipped open the blade. The blade was pitted and dull, but still it was a beautiful tool. He really liked Vola's knife.

It was the one he'd used on his journey last year, the one he'd used to smear the blood oath on his calf as he swore that he would find Pax. He still had a scar from that slice. Sometimes he'd feel an itch there and wonder if a mosquito had flown up his jeans. He'd roll them up to find nothing but the tiny crescent asking him to remember.

Well, he needed to stop remembering.

He snapped the knife shut. And right there in the dim shed, he performed the penance. Three times in his mind's eye, he dropped the rock over the den entrance.

The memory of making his oath that day was strong, though. The penance wasn't enough. Here at his old home where he had lived with Pax, it wasn't nearly enough.

He knew what would be. A penance with a new final scene, a scene he was always too chicken to force on himself, the thing his father said he should have done: put the kit out of its misery. His father, he knew, would have used a gun. Quick and neat. But Peter had been only seven years old. Maybe he would have been strong enough to drop the heavy capstone directly on the little kit. Life out immediately. Much more humane.

Bile rose into his throat the first time he did it. He spat it out, gritted his teeth, and ran it again. *Do it, walk away, don't look back.*

He wiped his eyes and went through it a third time.

Even that didn't feel like enough.

You couldn't go around some things, Jade had said. You had to go through them.

And right then, Peter saw clearly what that meant. It meant he had to go back to the scene of it all — the old rope mill. He had to stand on the spot where he'd let Pax go, and where he'd said goodbye to his father. Tonight he would sleep in this house, go through that. Then tomorrow morning he would walk to the mill site and feel all that loss, go through it and come back out. And then finally he could start over.

31

Pax lay in the shelter of the hemlock, curled around his kit. He ached whenever he moved, and he could tell by the way his daughter whimpered that she was bruised as well.

Time and stillness would heal them. Soon they would travel west to the Broad Valley and then north back to Bristle, as long as the human-set fires were out. Until then, except for the few steps to drink from the river, they would rest here as motionless as possible.

But the kit was restless. She twitched and squirmed and this caused her pain. She became irritable, and Pax could not distract her.

Until he noted where they were. *We are very close to the place I lived with my boy.*

The kit stilled. *Not dangerous?* she questioned again.

Not this one. He shared his home with me.

At that, the kit grew curious. *Den?* she wanted to know. *Like foxes?*

Den. Not like foxes. Aboveground. Then Pax described the vast box Peter and his father lived in, with other nest boxes inside. About the hard walls and slippery floors.

Not dirt? Not like foxes?

Not dirt. Not like foxes. Then he astonished her with a report of brooms, which were used to *remove* dirt from human homes. She was surprised at the permanence he described, also. How the human homes did not change, as fox homes changed with the seasons and with their travels. How humans slept in these homes under fair skies or storms.

Not like foxes?

Not like foxes. And the dens are not only for sleep. Inside, they rest and play also, they cook food.

They hunted in their nest boxes?

Not hunted. This was a mystery to Pax as well. The humans did not catch game, and their fruits and vegetables did not come from trees or land, they just appeared.

The kit curled closer to her father. She wanted to hear again about how he had come to live with the humans.

And Pax told the story of how he'd been rescued, taken from one home and carried to another.

Were you afraid? she wanted to know.

Pax considered. *I was not afraid when he brought me to his den and made me well. But after that, I was often afraid.*

And so you ran from him?

Pax dropped his head to rest it over his daughter's. His throat cupped her fragile skull. His own strong heart beat against her narrow spine. *I was never afraid that my boy would hurt me. After I loved him, I was often afraid that he would be hurt, or lost to me.*

You can love a human?

Yes.

And that makes you afraid?

Yes, after loving, you are afraid, Pax confirmed. *Like foxes.*

32

Following the path to the old mill was like following himself as a kid. Peter could almost hear his friends' dares when he passed the place where a pair of snarling guard dogs used to strain at their chains. At the driveway to the tall-gabled house, abandoned long before the war, he half expected to hear their voices cry out, *We don't believe in witches!* along with his. And he almost patted his pockets for an apple, passing the split-rail fence where the dapple gray pony used to wait.

Once in the woods, which still looked the same as before the war, the feeling was even stronger. There was the black walnut he and his friends had climbed to the very top, their initials carved in its bark. There was the loblolly where Peter had to bite his tongue every time, because just behind it was a tiny dell where jack-in-the-pulpits bloomed in March, and his mother had made him swear never to tell anyone, they were that scarce.

These things he remembered were only a few moments from his life. Where had all the other moments gone? And where were those boys now, dispersed by the war and the bad water? Would any come back to their empty town?

Without enough warning, Peter emerged from the wooded path. His eyes were drawn up immediately to the mill and the ridge above. "Jade said I was brave enough," he reminded himself out loud.

Maybe he was. But he needed a moment. He turned his gaze down to the river.

The first thing he noticed was that it had breached its banks and spilled a good ten feet wider at each side. It must be fifty feet across now. Sixty in some places.

Its surface was glassy flat this morning, except for a rolling furrow of current that flowed down the center. Its waters gleamed the same mirror-blue as the sky, looking so pure it was hard to believe what Jade had said — that poisons leaked from the things that had happened here.

He looked upriver. The rapids still tumbled, though much tamed today. As the falling water hit the bottom, it leveled out over deep pools. Peter knew those pools from the bottom up, had seen sky through them. A view that as a boy he always found disorienting but peaceful at the same time, as though time had relaxed.

A huge dead oak had snagged on the wreck of the mill wheel, spanning the river. Half-submerged, its roots seemed lifted in prayer over the far bank. Across the river, he recognized the rock where a year ago he'd found the carcass of a fox that for one terrible moment he had feared might be Pax.

A few yards up from that rock towered a giant hemlock, its boughs skirting the ground a good twenty-five feet across. If he were still a kid, Peter and his friends would swim across and storm that hemlock, claim the space under that skirt for a secret hideout. But he was not a kid anymore. It was a long time since he'd been a kid.

He turned toward the old mill. All the way up, the meadow seemed almost defiantly alive. Blossoms shot out of tall, bright grasses and even burst from the outcroppings of ledge. His mother had taught him the names of the wildflowers in the vicinity and he picked out a few now: bluebells and columbine and a crisp white blossom called bloodroot. That one was well named, he thought, springing out of this bloody soil.

Peter started climbing. He passed the spot where his father had run down to meet him and he kept going until he was inside the crumbling walls of the old mill. Here, the troops' tents had been set up. He and his father had gone into one and sat on his cot that last day. They had talked for an hour in a way they never had before.

He found a spot where that cot might have been, and he sat down.

Mostly his father had apologized. He'd regretted a lot of things. Peter had been so shocked that a bunch of the apologies had washed over him. But he heard the last one: "I'm sorry I made you leave that fox of yours alone by the side of the road in a place that wasn't safe. There must have been a better way."

In response, Peter told his father he'd found Pax just up on the ridge. And that there he had set Pax free himself, which was the truth. And then he'd said, "So it was okay, making me do that," which was a lie.

And then he'd steeled himself and given his father the hard news that he wasn't going back to his grandfather's. That he had found a place where he felt more at home, and wanted to live there until the war ended. "She isn't family, but I feel . . . I'm good there. I'm right there."

Surprisingly, his father hadn't been angry. "That's okay. If you feel good there, safe, then she's family enough."

Something about the words sounded familiar, as if they'd come from someone else, but Peter didn't have time to place them. Because then his father promised that things would be different when this was over. "I'll be a better parent."

Peter's answer to that came without thought. "You were a good father." Which was both true and not.

Clear as anything, he could still see his father's face: military-short hair, shaving cut on his cheek, beseeching eyes that filled with relief at those words. That was the last time Peter had seen him. He was glad it had ended there, with his father looking as if he'd been forgiven.

Peter stood up. He climbed the rest of the hill, up to the top ridge of trees and then over to the clearing Pax had led him to.

Here, he had chased off two coyotes who had treed another fox. And here he had set Pax free.

He sank down under the sweet gum tree in the center.

Which of the *last times* was harder? With his dad, not knowing it was the last time? Or with Pax, knowing?

He looked over to the rim of juniper that surrounded the clearing, located the exact spot he'd thrown the toy soldier — this time, feeling that Pax knew what he was doing. Every day since then he'd wondered if he'd done the right thing, sending Pax into the unforgiving wild, where he belonged but where he wasn't prepared to be, in the company of a burnt-tailed vixen.

If only he could know Pax was all right.

Peter wiped his eyes. He had done enough remembering for one day. He had felt his way into grief and maybe felt his way a few steps back out. He wished he could talk to Jade about it. He could almost see her pointing down at the river and sharing one of her metaphors about water.

He started down the hill. Halfway down, just as he turned for the path to home, he caught a glimpse of something copper across the river — a color that always arrested him.

A fox. Sitting beside the rock below the ancient hemlock. Adult, big. Male, probably. Healthy-looking. Watching him.

The fox was too far away for Peter to check for Pax's exact shading, or the single tear in the left ear. He couldn't feel the springy fur his fingers knew, or smell the outdoor oak-leaf smell his pet carried indoors. He couldn't hear his rumbling purr or yip of greeting. But he knew, from a sense deeper than those.

"Pax!" he yelled, starting to run before he could convince himself he was acting crazy. "Wait!"

33

Pax recognized his boy. Even though Peter's voice was deeper and his frame was taller, even after a year, he knew him.

He barked and sprang for the bank as Peter came flying down the hill on the other side of the river.

But just as Pax was poised to dive in, he heard a frightened cry from his kit. He took one more look at his boy and then hurried back to join her under the hemlock tree.

The kit had been terrified, waking at the close shout of a human and finding herself alone. Pax's presence comforted her, but when Peter's call came again, she startled.

That is my boy. He is not dangerous. I will visit him across the river while you sleep.

The kit pressed close to him.

You are not alone when I am out of sight.

Still, the kit looked up anxiously as Peter called again.

Pax guided her to the edge of the hemlock skirt. *You can watch from the shore.*

But the kit did not want to travel out. She bit at her left hind leg, which was trembling, and then she relieved herself — only a small splash — and crawled back inside. She curled up on the bed of soft needles, flicked her tail clean, and then curled it over her nose.

Pax settled himself beside his daughter while Peter's calls grew fewer and then ceased. At last, the kit closed her eyes. Pax waited until he was sure she was asleep, then he returned to the riverbank.

But his boy was gone.

The next day, once the kit had fallen into her heavy morning-sleep, Pax crossed the river. At the last spot he had seen his boy — halfway down the slope between the old mill and the river — he sat down. The sun was bright, the air mild, the breeze from the west so he would scent any danger to the kit. Pax waited.

And soon his old friend emerged from the wooded trail.

Pax shivered with pleasure. He leaped up and ran, barking. He rubbed his cheek against Peter's leg to refresh their bond. When Peter dropped to his knees and threw his arms around Pax, he returned the embrace with a hard push into his boy's chest, feeling the heartbeat he used to know as well as his own. Then he inspected Peter to reassure himself that his boy was well.

After the greeting of hugs, they played. The running and falling game. The wrestling game. The hiding and finding game, all the old games. Their familiarity was a joy.

But then something unfamiliar happened. Panting from running, Peter gulped water from a jug and then poured some into his cupped hand and held it out to Pax, urging him with a concerned voice. When Pax did not drink, Peter grew upset. Over and over he poured water and offered it until finally Pax took some.

After that, they lay side by side in the meadow. Peter stretched out with his chin propped on his fists; Pax tucked his paws beneath his chest. The sun warmed their backs as their breaths became calm again with grassy air. Both of them kept their heads turned toward the river — Peter's face intent, as if he were trying to understand something in its movement, Pax keeping watch on the hemlock just above the bank, where his kit slept.

Sometimes, Peter reached over to pluck pine needles from Pax's fur, and Pax loved this grooming that Bristle would have done. Sometimes, Peter's hand drifted over to scratch Pax's ears, a pleasure Pax hadn't felt in a year. Once, the surprising salt water streamed from Peter's eyes. He wiped his face and then rested an arm over Pax's shoulders for a long time. But mostly what Peter did was vocalize — much more than he used to — in a variety of tones, from pleased to distressed. Pax contributed a companionable grunt or purr when his boy seemed to want it, but otherwise was quiet.

Until the moment when he sensed his kit wake across the river.

Pax jumped up and barked to her. He took off at a run, and he did not look back.

34

Around midnight, Peter dragged his mattress off the bed and shoved it out the window. It was a trick he came up with when he first had Pax and couldn't sleep for worrying if the little fox kit was okay alone in his pen outside. Back then, he had to be sneaky about it and risk discovery in the morning if he didn't wake in time, but tonight he let the mattress thump onto the porch, then climbed out after it with a blanket.

He lay down and closed his eyes, but he still couldn't sleep.

The day had been wonderful — at least the hour he'd spent with Pax had been wonderful. That wasn't what was keeping him up. It was the argument about what to do next.

On the one hand, now he knew: Pax was alive. He was thriving in the wild. Peter could let go of all that guilt. And he'd learned his lesson about getting attached. Only a fool would go back to the river and call for Pax tomorrow, start the old danger up again, and Peter was finished being a fool.

On the other hand, it had been a long, long time since he'd spent such a fine hour. Peter had apologized as best he could and had felt Pax understood and forgave him. It had been good to be together again. It had felt like filling his cup.

He lay back and allowed himself to recall every minute.

He almost hadn't gone. He'd been sure it was Pax he'd seen the day before, but he'd called and waited for half an hour with no other sign of him. Maybe he'd fooled himself. All the way to the river, he'd talked himself down from any hope. Even if it was Pax, he might not show up again. And if he did, he was a wild fox now. He would be wary, and he had every right to be.

But when Peter came out of the woods, Pax was there, sitting in the middle of the field, just as if he'd been expecting him.

Peter had approached cautiously, hands out low, because like a dog, Pax liked to sniff at strangers' hands before deciding to bolt or stay. His heart had sped up as Pax rose. He'd figured Pax might need to come near, then back away, testing and deciding, but Pax had merely bounded over as though they'd been apart for a day, not a year. He licked Peter's hand eagerly, then leaned against his thigh, the gesture that meant he'd like Peter to scratch his head.

Shocked, Peter had. "What? Just like that? I'm forgiven?" he'd asked. "You don't have to make me pay?"

Pax rubbed his cheek against Peter's jeans. Peter knew this meant that Pax was marking him as his own. So apparently, yes, just like that, he'd been forgiven. The forgiveness had been a physical relief. He felt as though he'd been collecting rocks all year, carrying more and more on his back, and then all at once they'd crumbled to dust.

As Peter had examined his old friend, Pax had leaned in to sniff at his neck and shoulders, his face, as if he was doing the same thing. Peter had laughed out loud at that. "You're wondering if *I'm* okay? I'm okay!" He stroked Pax's ruff. "Do I seem different? Because you do."

Although it was hard to say exactly how. Pax wasn't any bigger, but somehow he seemed more rugged. His coat was definitely thicker, maybe shinier. He was obviously healthy.

Tears of relief had risen. "You're okay," he'd whispered, forehead pressed to Pax's. "I'm so sorry about what I did, but look at you — you came out okay."

They'd played then — the old games, and Pax remembered them. Thirsty afterward, Peter had taken a drink from his thermos and the realization had struck: if Pax lived near here, he was drinking this poisoned water. Pax was an adult, but still.

He'd poured out a handful for Pax. "The water here is bad now, but don't worry, it will be fixed. It will be clean and pure again after the Water Warriors."

For a second Peter had thought about how good it might feel to be part of the restoration here. Now it was personal, and now he would have this new, good memory of Pax, not the old, sad one. Maybe.

He offered his handful of water, again and again, until at last Pax drank some.

After that, they rested together. In front of them, the river ran with a quiet murmur. Peter watched it intently, trying to imagine what Jade would see in it — some wisdom, some helpful advice. But all he found were questions.

"There's so much I want to know," he'd said to his old pet. "Those first days — how did you learn to hunt? Where did you sleep? Was that you Jade saw at the reservoir? Do you have a family now?" More than ever before, Peter wished that Pax could talk to him. "Why are you here? Were you looking for me? Did you know somehow that I was coming?"

Pax had seemed to listen, and when Peter had told him how sorry he was, it had felt as if his fox forgave him.

But then Pax had suddenly jumped up, barked, and left without looking back. Except for the faint depression in the grass beside him, Pax had left no trace of his visit.

Now, lying on the porch at midnight, Peter thought about blame and forgiveness again. Maybe they were only human inventions. He remembered again the moment his father had asked to be forgiven, and the relief in his eyes when Peter had done it and the relief Peter had felt, too. For a second he wished he could see Jade again to ask her about these things. But that wasn't going to happen.

Suddenly everything he was thinking about seemed cowardly. Look at Pax. Pax had been hurt far worse than Peter by what had happened last year, but he had shown up. He had given himself over to whatever would happen. It felt as if his only question had been *Do I want to see Peter?* and the answer had been *Yes*, so he'd gone. No drama, no cowardly worry about what might happen.

But did that make Pax foolish or wise?

Peter realized he was doing it again, fretting over things he could just feel. The only question now was, *Do I want to see Pax again?* And the answer was *Yes*.

He would go back tomorrow.

35

For the next two days, when he heard Peter call — each time in the morning while his kit slept — Pax bounded out and swam across the river. They hugged and they played, and Pax accepted the water Peter insisted he drink, and they rested side by side. Until Pax heard his daughter awaken.

Then he jumped up and barked and left at a run.

Each day, Pax begged his kit to eat, and each day she refused, even the second day when he'd made the trip to the Broad Valley and brought back a mouse. She wanted eggs, and there were none here.

Each day, he brought her to the river to drink, and each day she drank.

Each day, she slept more.

Each day, she grew weaker and less steady on her feet, just as she had at the still pond.

36

For two days, Peter visited with Pax at the river in the mornings and worked on his home in the afternoons.

The chores inside the house were hardest, because memories seemed to grab for his throat from every corner of every room he entered. *What used to happen in here?* The question seemed printed in the air of every room.

On the first day, he'd walked into his father's room to look for a windbreaker and been ambushed by a brutal vision.

His father, that day he'd gone around collecting all his mom's belongings, eyes brimming, face purple, pulling her clothes from this closet. Himself, at seven years old, understanding only that this man was all he had now and therefore whatever he did was to be accepted. He didn't want to help — he couldn't have, anyway, his arms were frozen to his sides — but he'd followed room to room, watching the pile grow higher and higher.

That night, Peter had crept down to the basement where the pile had ended up. He'd slipped a few things out and hidden them: a pair of her favorite kneesocks, candy-cane-striped; a phoenix bracelet; some peppermint tea bags; a drawing he'd done for her birthday.

He'd always been grateful he'd saved those items. He'd given Vola the bracelet, but the other things were in his duffel bag right now, and would be heading down the river soon with the Water Warriors transport.

Peter dropped to the armchair in the corner, the windbreaker forgotten, and looked around the room, wondering what things of his father's he should keep. The watch he wore when he got dressed up. His tool belt. The cookie tin full of poker chips his dad had prized, but whose story Peter couldn't remember.

He was tempted again by the thought of a fire. Maybe he should put away these few special things, then burn everything else in the room. The idea upset him, so he ran back into the living room, where he was confronted by the fact that he still needed a jacket.

Each afternoon, after an hour of this kind of emotional warfare, his breath would be coming in short hard gulps and he'd have to run outside.

Even though there was more work to be done there, harder work, he liked being in the yard better. Outside, it was easier to look forward, harder to look back.

What he liked best was reclaiming his mother's vegetable garden. No one had touched it in the six years since she'd died, and the first afternoon he broke the hoe hacking out weeds as thick as his wrist, and had to switch to an axe.

Here he would grow his own food, the way Vola did. Maybe he'd even put in a few fruit trees around the perimeter like she had: peach and apple. His mother would have approved — she was always proud of her little crops. He'd bring her flower garden back, too. Just because.

The work outside was physically demanding, but it left headspace for worries.

Gardens cost money. He had a little cash with him, plenty for seeds at least, if he could find a place to buy them. He'd need a few tools, fertilizer, that kind of stuff. If he wanted to eat in the winter, he'd better get himself some jars, maybe a freezer for when the power came back. Until then, he'd have to build a cookstove. He collected water from the falls each day, but he should look for a closer source, at least until the groundwater was cleaned. And on, and on, and on.

Both evenings, he found himself slumped on the porch steps, head in his hands, near tears. Making everything worse, a garden's food was far in the future, and he needed something to eat right now. He had a cup of cornmeal left and a handful of dried apples.

Each night, he went to bed with a head full of problems and a belly full of hungry.

But both mornings, he woke up oddly excited.

"It's just a visit," Peter reminded himself each day, careful not to entertain any stupid ideas about Pax coming back to live with him again. "He's wild and better off that way." Still, the time he spent at the river with Pax was the best part of each day. Just some company. Just filling his cup. He would never be in a position to betray Pax again, so it was okay.

37

The next morning, a cold wind blew up before dawn. It whipped the blossoms off the redbuds, churned the river, and ruffled even the heavy hemlock boughs. It did not wake the kit, but it brought a welcome surprise to Pax.

He edged his muzzle out from their nest to be sure. Yes, a visitor — unanticipated, but much longed for. He quivered, his tail wagging faster and faster until a moment later, he burst out of the brush and tore down the hill to meet Bristle's brother.

Runt returned the joy in Pax's greeting, and the two play-wrestled the way they had since the very first day they had met.

My family? Pax wanted to know afterward, as they lay side by side in the sun, scenting each other for news.

Bristle was healthy, Pax was comforted to learn, and the kits as well. They wanted him to come back.

There is no longer any need to find a new home, Runt reported. *The humans have left the reservoir.*

Pax knew this, but he was surprised that Bristle did not worry the humans would come back. Then Runt shared news that astonished him even more: before they left, the humans had poured vast sheets of fish into the reservoir, so plentiful that even the kits could easily scoop them up. *It is safe at the Deserted Farm now, food is abundant. But Bristle was so grieved at losing her daughter that she won't leave the other two kits alone to hunt now. She needs you.*

Pax saw that Runt was also greatly sorrowed by the belief that his niece had died. *She is not dead. She is with me.*

Runt jumped to his feet. He had tracked the little vixen to the still pond, but after that, only Pax's trail led to the river, and

221

then that disappeared. He had picked up Pax's scent at the Broad Valley and followed it here. *Show me.*

Pax led him up the hill and under the hemlock bough. Runt barked his excitement at seeing his niece, and the kit awoke. She strained to rise to her uncle but fell back. She clasped his neck when he bent to cover her face in kisses.

Then Runt's brow pricked in concern. He pulled back and sniffed her carefully. *Unwell?*

Unwell, Pax confirmed.

Runt continued his distressed examination. *And small. Her brothers have grown larger.*

The kit pricked her ears at this news of her brothers.

The slight one is tall now, and quick. The other is still stocky and twice the size of this one. And they are strong. Runt related a game of ambush they liked to play with him, the heavier one jolting up suddenly beneath his belly, the rangy brother leaping onto his back. *They are constantly tumbling and leaping and testing their mother's patience.*

The little kit followed with rapt delight. Pax heard of her brothers' adventures with pleasure, too. But also with a splinter of anxiety.

He gazed down at his daughter. She was awake less and less each day. She seemed even frailer now, her chest rising shallowly with each breath. Her left paw, curled to her throat, trembled.

Runt dropped down beside her and wrapped his brush around her and she began to purr.

Pax darted outside. His daughter needed to eat. He would see that she ate today. He hunted for a few minutes in frustration, but found nothing but an earthworm.

When he brought the meal in, she turned away.

Pax left again and brought in a few moldy acorns.

The kit snuggled closer to her uncle and refused the morsel.

She wants eggs, Pax reported to Runt. *There are no eggs here. No game at all.*

There are eggs at the Broad Valley. And at the deserted farms. We'll travel home together now, Runt urged. *Bristle is waiting.*

Were there fires on your journey? Pax wanted to know.

Charred land, but no fires.

Pax watched his daughter struggle to her feet. She stood wavering at the edge of the little shelter, and he knew that she would try, but she could not make the trip.

He licked her ears with care and settled her down on the soft pine duff again. *You return,* he answered Runt. *We will follow when she is well.*

He walked with Runt to the edge of the shelter. *Stay,* he ordered his kit. *I will travel with Runt to the Broad Valley and bring back eggs. Do not go out.*

The kit's eyes widened at his strict tone, and then she dropped her head onto her paws again. And Pax was satisfied — it was nearly full morning, the time when she was sleepiest, so she would probably not wake until he returned. Still, he did not want to be away for long.

Hurry, he encouraged Runt once they were outside.

But Runt walked down to the riverbank and drew up short by the big rock.

Pax joined him. They were on the spot where Gray had died. Both foxes grew still, as if the calm that the old fox had always borne still rose from his bones.

Pax thought briefly of his boy, who would be coming soon. They would not visit together today. And then, standing shoulder by shoulder with his friend, he shared Runt's memories of what had happened here: Runt's triumphant splash across the water upon locating Bristle and Pax; his joyous sprint up the hill toward them, arrested halfway by the explosion that tore his leg from his hip; the days he'd lain near-dead in the muddy reeds, where he'd finally awoken to discover his terrible loss.

A fresh gust of cold ruffled the dark water. *Leave this place*, Runt urged. *Come home.*

38

On the third day, Peter woke up to a wind so sharp he heard it whistle through the backyard trees. He could feel a chill through the walls, as if winter were poking its fingers in, a little reminder it would come back. He should check the firewood supply today, he thought, pulling up the blanket.

And he remembered something: he knew where the key to the neighbor's back door was hidden.

The neighbor had been an old woman who lived alone, and he knew where the key was because he used to bring her firewood in for her. He knew something else: she had a pantry. An actual room just for food. She used to tell him, "Hurricanes, tornadoes, plagues, and wars — I've seen them all. Sane person is prepared."

When he'd finished stacking her firewood, she'd always tried to feed him — said she missed feeding her long-grown son. Since the first time, he always refused a meal, because all she wanted to talk about while he ate was how awful it was for a mother not to see her son, and that made it hard to swallow, what with the words *It's pretty awful the other way around, too* blocking his throat.

He threw on some clothes, grabbed the water jug, and ran down the middle of the empty road, wondering how long it would take him to get used to watching for cars again. He knocked on the back door out of habit, then, after a minute, let himself in.

The old woman must have left in a hurry. A blouse was hung over a sofa arm, a threaded needle still in it; a crossword magazine lay open on a coffee table; dishes were crusted in the sink. Everything was hazed with dust.

He opened a door off the kitchen and there it was. A mess — it stank of mice, and oats and flour were strewn across the floor — but there were still shelves full of neatly lined-up cans and jars. Jams and soups, dried milk, fruits and vegetables . . . even peanut butter, three jars.

He was going to be okay. There was enough here to feed him until he figured stuff out. And it wasn't stealing, because she was always offering it to him. And if she returned after the water was restored, he'd find a way to pay her back. He'd even listen to her complaints about missing her son. As long as she wanted to talk, he would listen.

Tonight he'd come back with a wheelbarrow and load up. But right now, he had a friend waiting.

A friend who loved peanut butter.

Peter jammed a jar into his pocket and headed out.

The sun was high overhead when he reached the river, its waters whipped into waves. He called, loud across the wind, "Pax! Sorry I'm late!"

Ten minutes went by. No Pax. Peter opened the peanut butter, wondering how far the smell went, waved it around.

After another ten minutes passed with no sight of his fox, Peter went up the hill to collect his water. Then he came back and settled on a ledge of rock halfway down the meadow to wait, jar of peanut butter in his hand.

He kept an eye on the scrubby undergrowth just down from the huge hemlock, where Pax had emerged the past two days. The reeds downriver were rustling in the wind, making a peaceful sound. He was tired, and his eyes kept drifting closed, so he almost missed it.

A shift at the base of the undergrowth. Something pointed and brown poked out — maybe a face, maybe not — then disappeared. Peter watched carefully, and after a minute, he saw it again.

Yes, a furred face, cinnamon colored. But small — far too small to be Pax. The animal moved. Glimpses of bright fur through the shrubs. Peter strained to see — a puppy, maybe? What was a puppy doing way out here, where no people lived?

Whatever it was made its way toward the water and then emerged: a fox kit, two months old at most, very thin.

Peter sat up. The kit wobbled down the path to the bank. And in slow motion he put it together: she was going to drink from the poisoned water.

He jumped off the ledge and started to run, Jade's warning sounding in his head like an alarm. *The young are most at risk, developing nervous systems.*

"Get away!" he shouted. "Go!"

The kit jumped at his voice. It froze for a moment, but then it took a cautious step into the rocky shallows.

Peter slid down the bank. He could see the little fox more clearly now. It had fluffy copper fur and a sharp, delicate face. A vixen, probably. Where was her mother? "Get away!" he yelled, louder. "Go on! Go!"

The kit staggered, but she didn't turn back. She lowered her head to drink.

And Peter didn't think. He hurled the jar in his hand, and even as he released it he knew: his throw was too hard, his aim too straight. *Run*, he willed the kit, but she didn't and the jar exploded right where she stood.

Just then, a large fox tore out of the undergrowth.

Pax leaped into the shallows and snatched up the kit — *his* kit, Peter understood at once.

"I'm sorry! I wasn't trying to hurt her!" Peter yelled, splashing into the river. But Pax and his daughter had disappeared.

39

As soon as he'd carried her under the hemlock boughs, Pax checked his kit thoroughly. He could find no injury; still, his heart beat fast with dread. *You left this safe spot*, he scolded.

I was thirsty. The kit did not lower her body in submission, but she wagged her little brush, asking pardon for her disobedience.

Pax licked her cheeks to show she was forgiven.

You said your boy was not dangerous. But he threatened.

No. There was no threat. Pax was certain of that, but he was also puzzled. Peter had hurled something that had smashed on a rock right next to his daughter. Why?

Often, his boy used to throw a white leather orb at another boy, who caught it in a thick covering he pulled onto one hand. Over and over, Peter threw. The throws were hard, like the one at the river, but both boys laughed and were at ease when they played this game.

Those times were different from today, though. Pax remained puzzled. *My boy meant no harm. He felt sadness and concern.*

The kit wanted to know how he could tell this with the wind blowing away from the boy.

This Pax could explain. *He called to us in his grief-yearning tone.*

His grief-yearning tone?

Pax reflected on the many times he had heard this tone from his boy.

He'd heard it most often when Peter sat alone in his nest room. It had been strong the final days he'd seen his boy last year: when Peter had packed his possessions into a box; when he'd wailed as the car peeled away; when he'd sent Pax away the day with the coyotes.

233

But Pax shared a different memory with his kit. One from his earliest days with Peter.

I was in my pen, hungry. My boy had not fed me that night. There had been angry shouting between him and his father in the afternoon and he had run away, and had not come home by sunset.

I grew anxious, pacing my pen.

He came back so late the moon was high. He brought my food. He sat beside me as I ate, soothing me in his grief-yearning voice. My boy lay down in the straw bedding with me, and even in sleep, the grief-yearning scent hung on him all night. It is both sorrow and want.

Still, the kit did not understand.

It is like the grief call of foxes. Pax had shared this cry with the skulk of foxes when Gray died, and with Bristle when Runt had gotten hurt. But he understood that his kit had never heard it. *You will know that call. But humans alone know the grief-yearning.*

Before he could explain further, they were surprised by a commotion of crows landing in the branches above them.

Pax slipped out to listen.

The huge group of humans, the ones from the reservoir, were back, he learned. They were moving down the river again.

How far? How fast? Pax wanted to know. But the crows flew on, rising so suddenly the boughs clicked with their release.

Pax ducked back inside. *We must leave. Can you walk?*

The kit got up. She followed Pax out, setting off at a strut, but after a few steps, she lost her balance.

She looked down at her back leg, as if offended that it would not serve her. She shook herself and sneezed out some leaf litter, then lifted her chin and set out again.

And once more, she crumpled.

Pax came to her side. He examined her more closely.

No stingers blistered her skin, as when Bristle had nosed out a hive of bees. She had no weeping wound, was not in pain, like Bristle when her tail had been burned. Her belly was not rigid, as Runt's had been after eating greened potatoes at the deserted farms. She was not wounded so badly she fell into a sleep from which she could not awaken, as Runt had been when he had lost his leg.

Bristle and Runt had gotten better each day from those injuries.

His kit was weakening the way he himself had been weakening in the days before remembering: growing more ill each day. He would have died if the boy Peter hadn't taken him in.

He looked down at his kit. He knew, finally, what to do. He lifted her by the scruff of the neck and felt how light she was, how loose her skin was.

Home? the kit asked.

I will see you safe, was Pax's promise.

40

"Stupid. Stupid, stupid," Peter muttered as he walked around the backyard, picking up deadwood and laying it in a circle on the bare spot where the driveway ended. He was cursed. Everyone he loved, he hurt. Hadn't he learned that?

He opened Pax's old pen and swept up an armload of moldering straw, exposing mouse tunnels and scuttling beetles. He ran out and tossed the straw over the wood, shouting louder, "Stupid, stupid!" and went back for more.

He hurt everyone, and then they were gone. His mother, on the last day of her life, so disappointed in him. He'd told Jade about it, and Jade had said that he wasn't to blame because he was only seven, and besides, mothers didn't have car accidents because their kid smashed a garden globe. But what did Jade know?

His father. Look what happened to him. A hundred miles from base? He was probably traveling to Vola's, because in spite of what he'd said, it must have hurt him that Peter was living there. Peter had avoided facing this truth, but what else could his father have been doing?

And Vola. For the rest of his life, he would see the wounded look on her face when he'd told her that he didn't need her, that she wasn't his mother.

And now Pax. *Again.* Last year should have been enough, but no, he'd set himself up to betray his old pet again. He hoped Pax had heard the regret in his voice as he'd screamed, *Sorry!* but that was wishful thinking.

Stupid, stupid, stupid.

But never again. He was starting over. Today he would do the brave thing and really end his old life, so he could begin a new one.

The ring of kindling now covered with straw, Peter ran inside, into his room. He tore the clothes out of the closet, ripped the posters from the walls, kicked boxes out from under the bed. He swept his shelf clear of photos and magic tricks, books and puzzles, geodes and arrowheads and little matchboxes filled with tiny animal skeletons. Everything crashed to the floor.

He scooped up a load of the old life of a stupid kid and carried it to the outside, threw it onto the ring of straw. Trip after trip, moving faster and faster, he stripped his bedroom until it was bare to the floorboards.

From the shed, he grabbed the lighter fluid, ran back outside, and doused the whole mess. Then he tore into the kitchen. He was panting now, but he didn't dare slow down or else he might not go through with it. He grabbed a box of matches, flew back outside, struck one and tossed it.

The fire burst to life with a roar that kicked the breath out of his chest.

And everything he'd been holding tight for a year let go. As the fire ate his old life, he began to wail. When it raged, he howled. He pulled his shirt off to feel his skin sting in the searing heat. He crouched over the flames until he smelled the ends of his hair singe. He cried for all he had lost, including, finally, the father who was not where he should be in the house behind him. He cried and he cried, so close to the flames that the tears crisped his cheeks, and his eyes and throat were gritted with cinders.

Finally, spent, he climbed onto the porch and sank to the steps. Beside him, his backpack hung off the railing.

Maybe it should go, too.

His mother had bought it for him when he went to school, first grade. Maybe he should throw it on the fire. Because it held memories, too — Pax had crawled into it the first day he'd brought him home.

But it was a good pack. Plain navy blue, rugged canvas, full-sized. Year after year, he'd grown into this pack, until now it fitted his shoulders like a set of muscles. And he would need a good backpack going forward. Besides, his father's ashes were in it.

Peter pulled the pack off the railing and hugged it to his chest. As soon as the fire died down, he would bring his father's remains to the cemetery and spread them over his mother's grave. Today was a day for being brave, after all.

He left the backpack on the railing and turned back to the fire. And he saw what he had done.

A nest. He had built a nest and set it on fire with all the trappings of his old life. Exactly like the phoenix story. Instead of incense and spices, he smelled wool and paper and melted plastic and the rubber from his sneakers, but it was still the same story: new life, arising from the ashes of old.

The fire grew calmer, finishing its business in no hurry. Listening to it ruffle, Peter closed his eyes. It was funny how stories could travel through time. His mother had loved that phoenix myth and taught it to him — he could still remember her voice rise in excitement when she got to the do-over, fresh start of the story.

On the day he'd left Vola's to find Pax, he'd used it to get her to burn her old wooden leg, the one she'd dragged around as her own penance for what she'd done in the war. He had felt certain her punishment had outlasted its usefulness, and when he'd returned a few weeks later, he could see that it was healing her to wear the prosthesis and accept that her terrible debt was paid.

Later Vola had passed the story on to her friend the bus driver, who had his own demons. Who knew who might hear it after that guy, or who had been touched by it all those years before his mother heard it?

When he opened his eyes, he forced himself to watch the last of the mound crumple to ash. Only when the smoke cleared over the embers did he finally lift his gaze.

At first he thought it must be a heat mirage: Pax, sitting beside the shed. Hanging from his mouth was something small and furred.

Peter rubbed his sore eyes. It was no mirage. Pax was there, holding a fox kit in his jaws. Dead, it looked.

The jar must have hit Pax's kit after all. He had killed her. And Pax had come to say, *Look what you've done.*

He buried his face in his hands, like a coward. Then he remembered — this was his day for being brave. He uncovered his eyes to face what he'd done.

And then the kit squirmed.

Peter sat up.

Pax walked around the fire bed and right up to the steps, holding Peter's gaze all the way.

"I wasn't aiming for her . . . ," Peter started, then stopped. He could never explain. "What do you want, boy?"

As if in response, Pax placed the kit at his feet, where it looked impossibly small. The kit backed into the space between her father's forelegs, shivering.

Peter's hand reached out automatically to comfort the frightened kit, then he pulled it back and looked at Pax to see if that would be okay. When Pax didn't seem to object, he touched the little forehead with a single finger: skull bone, delicate as an egg, under silky fur. "What's going on? Do you want food for her, Pax? I have food."

Pax stepped over his daughter and leaned into Peter. He fitted his head into the space between Peter's jaw and his collarbone, the position he used to fall asleep in. Peter felt his old friend's soft breath warm his ear. Throat to throat, pulse to pulse, it was a position of trust, and Peter knew he was being forgiven again, which made him feel like weeping.

The kit mewed. She stretched up on her hind legs, and Pax bent to her. They rubbed muzzles.

And something passed between the father fox and the daughter, and Peter didn't need a translator. Pax was reassuring her, telling her that he loved her, that it was all right.

Then Pax shocked him by walking away.

Peter jumped up. "Where are you going?"

The kit scrambled after her father. But she wavered and tumbled over onto her left side. Her eyes panic-wide, she got up, but she fell again after a few steps. She wailed.

Pax stopped and turned at her cry, but he did not come back. He lifted his gaze to Peter.

And then Peter understood. "Oh, no. Not that! Come back!"

Pax walked to the edge of the yard, where the woods began, and then sat. It was clear what he was waiting for.

"I can't do it! I won't."

Still Pax waited.

Peter thought of his fox's easy trust, and he was washed with shame. "All right," he called. "I'll take her." He crouched and scooped up the little creature.

She was impossibly light, just bones and fur and wide, scared eyes, and she whimpered in a way that made Peter's heart squeeze. "Wait. Pax, come back! Please!" he called.

Pax stood and then disappeared into the woods.

Watching him leave, Peter felt abandoned. But also as if something had been completed. He had turned Pax out into the wild because he knew it was best for him. And now Pax was leaving his kit for the same reason. Because obviously that was true — Pax would never abandon his own baby unless he was desperate, unless it was for her own welfare.

He remembered his father's words upon hearing he wanted to stay with Vola: "She is family enough."

"You're a good father, Pax," he called after the friend he could no longer see. "But I don't think I'm family enough."

Peter looked down at the cowering fox kit in his cupped palms. *Had* he hit her? He looked her over, but could see no wound. He put her down. She backed away, but again she stumbled, as if her left legs weren't working well.

And all of a sudden he understood. "Oh, no." He scooped her up and tucked her under his chin as the full realization struck: the tremble, the balance problems Jade had described in the baby raccoons. "The water. You've been poisoned by the water."

For a minute, a crazy idea arose. Jade had talked about a treatment for cleaning out heavy metals: milk, charcoal, something else. Maybe he could do all that and then set the kit loose.

But no. Nothing would completely reverse the damage, she'd said. And out in the wild, a defect didn't have to be severe. Just a slight weakness would make a fox kit's survival nearly impossible.

His old self, before Pax, would have taken her to raise. But he wasn't that kid anymore. No, there was only one humane thing to do — the thing his father had said he should have done with Pax. "I'm sorry," he told the kit. "I promise I won't let you suffer. But I can't do it here. Your dad might be nearby, or he might come back."

Peter nestled the kit on top of the box of ashes in his backpack where she wouldn't be crushed, then shouldered it. He went into the shed and grabbed a spade, then into the basement workshop where his father kept a hunting rifle.

He had never managed to touch that rifle. For years, his father had tried to get him to learn to shoot it. Peter had always refused, because just the sight of it made him feel sick, reminding him of what his father had suggested about putting Pax out of his misery.

Now he reached out. He picked it up.

And spade in one hand, rifle in the other, he set out for the cemetery.

41

After only a few bounds, the urge to turn back for his kit grew too strong.

Pax stopped. He pushed into a stand of saplings and poked his head out.

He saw Peter put his kit on the ground, and his haunches flexed in readiness to run back to her.

But then Peter lifted the kit and cradled her under his chin. His boy crooned to his daughter in a tone of great care, and he held her close, and she ceased squirming.

Still Pax hesitated, torn.

But then Peter tucked the kit into his backpack.

At that, Pax felt his anxiety release. The pack was a sacred cache for his boy. Season after season, year after year, Peter kept that pack with him, worn close to his body. Pax himself had been sheltered there.

His daughter, he knew for certain now, would be safe.

Pax turned away. He began to run. He ran harder and harder. All through the day and all through the night, he would run. Until he reached the den under the shed at the Deserted Farm, he would run.

Not because of the pull of the foxes who loved him, waiting there.

Not because the coming summer, with its glorious abundance, sang all around him.

He ran because if he did not, his heart would shred.

42

Peter stood at the cemetery entrance, his legs suddenly rooted.

He'd walked here right down the middle of Main Street, unsettled the whole way to hear not even a single car. In another month, when the Water Warriors had finished their cleanup, people would start moving back. Things would be easier then. But also harder. As Jade had pointed out, thirteen-year-olds were not allowed to live by themselves. Another problem he'd have to figure out. But not today.

He pressed his face to the big iron gates and peered through the bars. The cemetery lawns, always clipped and weeded, had been untended now for a year. Rolling carpets of ragged green grass, spattered with dandelions and cornflowers, hugged the gravestones.

He pushed open the gates and climbed the path toward his mother's grave. It was so quiet, he heard every pebble crunch.

When he reached her headstone, nestled in the shade of a giant elm, he laid the gun and the shovel off to the side. He was relieved to see that the mountain laurel bush he and his father had planted was thriving, looking at home in the shaggy grass. "I like it better natural like this," he said aloud. "I think you would too."

Peter slipped the pack off his shoulders and placed it on the ground. From it, he withdrew the box of ashes, then zipped it back up. He opened the box and undid the tie on the bag inside. "I know you missed Mom, too," he said. "It was just hard for you to say it. So I think this is where you want to be."

He lifted the heavy bag high and tipped it open. The grit sifted over the grave gently as snow, and then the softer ash floated down. It seemed to melt into the stone and the long grass and the flowers, as if it had been waiting to be here all along.

Holding the empty bag, Peter felt tears course down his face again and he didn't even try to wipe them away. "I wish you were still here," he said to his parents, talking to them both at once for the first time in six years. "It's been a really hard day. And it's not over."

Peter took up the shovel. First, he cut out a disk of turf beside the mountain laurel so that when he buried the kit he could cover her with the peaceful grass. Then only a few shovelfuls of soft dirt and he had a hole deep enough that no scavenger would disturb it.

He picked up the rifle. When he lifted the wooden stock to his cheek, he felt it tremble. His legs felt weak, but he braced them wide. He tightened his grip and slid the bolt to chamber a cartridge, then shoved the bolt shut, the way he'd seen his father do dozens of times.

Then he knelt to the pack and tugged open the zipper with his free hand, not looking inside. He got back up and released the safety. Its click seemed to ricochet around the silent cemetery.

He lifted the rifle to his cheek again and aimed at the open backpack, his grip slick with sweat. He would pull the trigger the instant the kit emerged, before she could turn those golden eyes on him, so like Pax's. *Make it painless . . . the right thing to do . . .* He heard his father's words from all those years ago.

He nudged the backpack with a foot. The pack didn't move, and Peter wished irrationally for a second that somehow the kit had escaped. But then he heard a faint mew, like Pax's when he was little, and that sound hurt in his gut, and suddenly he had tossed the rifle and was retching behind the tree.

Afterward, he fell into the long grass, arms hugging his knees, panting. His eyes filled again, this time in shame. Here he was, hugging his knees and feeling sick, when all that was left of his father was gritty ash on the long-grown grass around him, waiting for him to grow up and do the right thing. He reached out for some of the ash, and as he looked at it on his fingertips, it struck him: here was proof. His father wasn't alive anymore. There would be no more making it better between them.

But also, there was no more making it worse.

He looked at the pack and imagined the kit shivering inside. And suddenly, he knew — maybe shooting her would have been the right thing for his father to do, but it wasn't the right thing for him. It didn't seem brave. It seemed cowardly, in fact. If that was a disappointment to his father, or to anyone, well, it didn't matter. It was his life, and he had to live it.

He crawled over to the pack. He peered in and the kit looked up at him, and he could see how frightened she was. He saw how large he must seem. How terrifying. "Come out here," he urged her softly. "I won't hurt you. I just need to see you to know what to do."

He got a grip around her chest, felt her heart pounding, and he pulled. He heard her claws scramble to catch hold of the canvas.

He tugged again, and she grabbed on more fiercely. She was a willful little thing, and even sick she was strong. He detached her, one paw at a time, as she wriggled and hissed, until finally he managed to draw her out.

Caught by one claw was a wrinkled brown envelope.

A chill went through him seeing that military insignia again. For two months, he had forgotten it was there.

Well, he'd already dug a hole. He would bury the letter here. Unread.

He pulled the envelope off and was about to drop it in the kit's grave when he thought, *No.* Maybe the report was better than he'd been fearing. Besides, today was his day for doing brave things. Wouldn't the brave thing now be to read it?

He sat back, corralling the kit with his legs, and shook open the brown envelope. Two white envelopes fell out. One official army correspondence, one plain and square.

The letter from the army had been opened. His grandfather, of course. *Your father died of stupid,* he'd warned. Peter pulled out the official report.

It was not better than he'd feared. It was worse.

His father was killed off-site, by enemy mortar, which Peter and his grandfather had known. The news was that his father had not been authorized to be off-site. That was bad — being marked as "away without leave" — but it wasn't the worst. They found rations in the jeep he'd taken, which amounted to theft of government property, and money, which implied he'd been deserting. Protocol demanded that his status be changed to *Dishonorable* to reflect that.

Peter tore up the letter and threw it into the kit's grave.

He picked up the other envelope. Obviously a card. A bunch of condolence cards had been sent to his grandfather, and Peter had read them. "Your son was a good man," and "It was an honor to serve with him," that kind of stuff. If the senders had known what was in the report, though, would they still have said that?

This envelope was addressed only *To His Son,* but his grandfather had opened it, too.

Well, if he was going to be brave today, he might as well go all the way.

Peter withdrew the card. It was blank. Tucked inside was a sheet of lined notebook paper. He unfolded it and read:

I saw you once. You came to the base here, on crutches, to see your dad.

After you came, he started hunting me down, to talk. See, I was about to be a father — twins — and I guess I went on about that, I was so proud.

I'm sorry I don't remember your name, but I should, because you are who he talked about. All the time. How tough you were — all those miles on crutches. He was proud of that. And that you were smart and kind like your mom. Said you had a way with animals, nearly magic, he said, and you shouldn't be without. He said he owed you for that, something about a lost fox, I don't remember.

Anyway, I know he would want me to tell you something: he didn't desert. He did go AWOL, but he didn't desert. And he had a reason. And the reason was me.

What happened was this: I hadn't heard from my wife in over a week. The babies were due soon, so I wanted to find out was she okay. I couldn't go home — nobody could get leave. I was scared to sneak out — not that it would be dangerous, there was no fire around, but with two babies coming, I couldn't afford to get discharged, lose my pay. Still, I was about crazy, so I decided to go.

Your dad, he said he knew something about worrying about a wife who goes missing one day.

So he went in my place. Four hours there, four hours back, he wouldn't even be missed, he said. He'd find out was she okay, give her some money and food I'd saved, and be back before reveille at dawn.

Except he wasn't. I figure you know that part.

So he didn't desert. He ran a mission for a friend. And now two babies have a father because you don't. And their father has a paycheck, which is not nothing.

I never told. I'll carry this shame my whole life, but I'm hoping you will keep my secret, because these two babies still need their father's paycheck. But I guess that's up to you.

I thought you should know the truth.

I am sorry,

Private Thomas Roberts

Peter sat motionless with the note open on his thigh, not seeing it. He heard bees working the cornflowers and the screech of a hawk, but he barely registered them. He wasn't really there. He was up by the mill, sneaking a jeep out — hot-wired, lights out, engine cut — risking a lot for a mission of kindness. Being a man.

On the last day, his father had said he would change. Sitting on Peter's thigh was proof that he had.

He looked over at his mom's headstone, wishing he could tell her. Her last words had been about his father: *Don't be like him*. But if she could read this letter, he knew she would say, *Be like him. Be just like him.*

Because that was how his father had changed — he had become the person she'd wanted him to be. And suddenly he realized something else: that last day, when his father had said, *That's okay*, about Vola, that he could stay with her, it had been his mother's influence he'd heard in the kind words.

"I messed up with Vola," he said aloud now to her stone. "I was mean to her. I think that's why I've been feeling like I failed you. She'd never take your place, but she would be something else, something good, and I think you'd be happy for me to be there."

He read the note again. This time, knowing what was coming, he wanted to yell at his father, *Don't do it! It's his wife, not yours, make him go himself!* and growing angry at this man who'd caused his father's death. But even as he did, he knew that was a little kid's anger, a little kid looking for someone to blame. He knew that.

He read the letter a third time. This time, at every sentence he felt pride — such a large, strange feeling that he felt his heart stretch to accommodate it.

But the sentence that struck him the hardest was his dad's wish. *Said you had a way with animals, nearly magic, and shouldn't be without.*

As he read that one over again, Peter realized with a shock that his fingers were stroking the thin neck of the kit, who had fallen asleep against his thigh. He pulled them back.

The kit awoke and gave a questioning whimper. She didn't sound frightened anymore. Just lonely.

Peter picked her up. She hung in front of his face, no longer struggling. She looked into his eyes so deeply it was as if she was searching for something at the back of his soul.

But Peter was the one who found it.

He pulled her to his neck. "I don't know what I'm going to do with you." He leaned over and slid the safety back on the rifle. "But it sure isn't this."

Peter got up and settled the kit into his pack again. He picked up the shovel and began to dig. He enlarged the little hole he'd dug, shoveling in a line, saving the turf, until he'd made a trench long enough.

Then he dropped in the rifle and covered it over with the soft dirt and the peaceful grass. The right thing for him.

43

Pax ran.

He traveled for two days without rest, so eager was he to make his way back to his family. But at the spot on the path where he could first see his home, he stopped short.

Two big glossy kits tumbled on tall, sturdy legs across the bowl of grass in front of the shed. Bristle lay on the step above them, relaxed but keeping watch, a patch of sun burnishing her shoulders to copper.

Pax climbed the boulder beside the path and sat. His sons were upwind and would not scent him, and in his amazement, he wanted a moment to just watch them.

They were well matched now. The bear-like one was still larger and could easily knock his brother to the ground. But the smaller one had grown tall, and he was agile. He could wriggle free and pounce before the larger one could turn around.

They were so different from the kit Pax had just left. Their movements were fluid, no longer clumsy, and they seemed tireless. Over and over they tumbled, all jump and swagger, growling and nipping in mock menace. And over and over they sprang apart, charmed by whatever wonders — swaying raspberry canes, crickets, their own tails — begged them to investigate.

Swelled with pride and love, Pax rose.

And at that same moment, Bristle's face turned toward his. Her ears perked, she flicked her tail. She bounded off the step, over her frolicking kits.

Pax leaped from the boulder at a run, too. He greeted his mate with glad nuzzles and barks, but instantly, the two big kits crashed into them, pawing and kissing their way to their father.

Bristle stepped back.

Up close to his sons, Pax was surprised again by how large and strong they had grown. They knocked into him, they sprang onto his back, pressing their muscles to his. Together, they made a show of pouncing on a pinecone as though it were a mouse, batting it between themselves. Then they took turns tearing off to show some other skill they'd acquired, then charging back to express more love.

At last they collapsed into a heap, panting against Pax's side in the sunshine.

Only then did Bristle rejoin her mate.

She bathed Pax, taking care over his ears, his whiskers, the cracked rib, the paws that had traveled so many miles for their family. She rubbed her cheek over him, mingling their scents.

As she did, Bristle found the traces of her daughter.

Through Runt she had learned that the little vixen was very ill. *She has died?*

No, she lives. Pax related all.

At first, Bristle was upset by the news that the boy, Peter, had her kit. But after Pax assured her that their daughter would not have survived the journey home, she quieted. Some humans were not danger-ous, she had learned. The ones at the res-ervoir had been peaceful. They had shared bounty. *You trust this human?*

I trust my boy.

He will care for her?

Yes. Pax was certain.

And Bristle took comfort.

But their family had been diminished by one.

Pax and Bristle led the grief call, and although the brother kits had never heard it, they had been born with the cry in their throats.

After a moment, Runt emerged and loped over to join them. Standing fur-to-fur, five foxes wailed, and the call sang of the absence that was theirs alone and of all the losses in the world. And it sang of the joy that remained.

44

Peter dropped his duffel bag. He stared at the little cabin.

A nest hung from one of the rafters, as if some bird were announcing what a nice place to live it was. The mountain laurel he'd planted by the cinder-block doorstep was fringed with new growth. The doorframe, such fresh green wood when he'd left, had already begun to weather in the six weeks he'd been away.

The urge to grab the doorknob and go inside was strong, but he resisted. This wasn't his home. Not yet.

He ran a hand along a couple of logs. All were straight and true. None had shrunk. Beneath the windowsill, though, he noticed a lump of daubing bulging out.

He pulled his jackknife from his back pocket and then paused. He couldn't help a quick smile. Samuel had loved the one Peter had given him — the twin to this one, his father's — all polished and sharpened like new. Jade had loved her wedding present, too — the candy-cane-striped wool socks his mother had treasured. But the real gift had been the way it had made Peter feel to share these mementos with people who would appreciate them. Not quite as if his parents were still alive, but as if they still mattered.

He flipped open his knife and chipped off the excess daubing.

And then he kept going. He dug out a fair run of chinking until he'd cleared a crack. Through it, he saw a slice of sun-polished floor inside. He could almost hear his home ease in a breath.

No. Not his home. Not yet.

He started off down the path. With each step, though, he grew more uncertain. How could Vola welcome him, after the way he'd left? After the terrible thing he'd said to her, which was a lie. And after that moment in the truck when she'd said that he felt like family, and he had bitten back the words that were the truth.

By the time he reached her granite doorstep, he was thinking about bolting again. But it was too late.

Vola was at the stove, stirring something in a pot. She turned to the screen door when he stepped up. Peter saw her bring her apron to her face and he wished he knew, was she just wiping away some flour, or was it tears? Because suddenly he felt close to crying.

And then she raised an arm and waved him in.

He slipped off his backpack, propped it against the doorframe, then pulled open the door and crossed the threshold.

Vola took a step toward him, and it felt as if the step were a question. "You're here."

"I am," he said. He took another step in, too, just as much a question.

Peter smelled peaches simmering with cinnamon, and butter browning. He was suddenly starving.

Which Vola seemed to guess. "Maybe I should set an extra place?" she asked casually.

"Maybe. Please."

"I should warn you: your grandfather is likely to show up."

Peter searched her face for meaning.

"Every Sunday afternoon, like clockwork. Says he's helping me out but, well . . . I let him say that. He's been reroofing the barn, always seems to finish up right around supper."

"He scores a meal with you every week?"

"He does. But it is not the food he's after. He brings the week's papers, all the articles about Water Warriors circled. He reads them out loud while I am cooking. Then he wonders what you might be up to. He'd be pretty excited to find a surprise guest here."

"Well, actually . . . two surprise guests. I brought someone with me."

Vola peered over his shoulder, out the screen door.

"No," Peter said, "not like that." He opened the door and lifted his backpack and brought it in. And Vola gasped at the curious little face poking out.

Peter freed the squirming bundle of bright copper fur. The kit licked Peter's face as if to reassure him she wouldn't get into trouble, then kicked to get down.

Peter set her on the floor and she immediately began a thorough investigation of Vola's foot and her prosthesis. She flicked her ears as if she found both satisfactory and then pranced off to explore the kitchen.

Peter laughed. "She has to know everything that's going on."

They watched the kit sashay around the kitchen. Beside the sink she came to a full stop. She rose on her hind legs, sniffing madly.

Peter laughed again. "Eggs on the counter. She loves them. Just like her father."

And it didn't hurt. For the first time in over a year, mentioning Pax didn't hurt. "You'll have to watch out — she can smell them a mile away. Every time I turned around, she had one of the Water Warriors feeding her an egg."

"She looks hungry," Vola said. "Better give her some."

Peter took a dish and cracked one of the eggs into it. Then he remembered Jade's kindness with the chickadee. He offered the dish to Vola. "You feed her," he said. "She's got to get to know you if we're going to live here."

Vola took the dish but she froze. "And so . . . are you, boy? Going to live here?"

And Peter finally said the words that he had bitten back. "You aren't my mother, but you feel like my family, too, Vola. I feel good here with you, and safe, and I need that and my parents would be happy about it. So if the offer's still open . . ."

"The offer? What offer?"

Peter's heart stuttered. "To be here for good. For this place to be my home. You said, I thought you said . . ."

"Oh, no, no, no. That was not an *offer*. I was *telling* you what I was going to do. Have papers drawn up. Which I did. The land is already yours."

And Peter's breath returned. Along with some tears he wiped away. "Thank you."

"You are going to stay," Vola said softly, as if it was a miracle. And then she was wiping her own face, and both of them smiled at that.

Just then, the kit gave a little yip that said she'd been ignored long enough. Vola put the dish down. She reached out a hand to stroke her back, then looked up at Peter.

"Go ahead," he told her. "She's good with people. Pax only knew me and my dad. He was skittish around anyone else. But this one's friends with about a hundred troops already."

After the kit cleaned the plate, she gave Vola's ankle a polite thank-you lick, then she took off again.

"Is she limping?" Vola asked.

"Just a little. It was worse before. You almost don't notice now, right?"

"She was hurt?"

Peter scooped up the little explorer, who was about to ambush a broom. "Poisoned. Heavy metals, we figured. From drinking from the river before we decontaminated it. A friend of mine, Jade, she helped me